THE COURTESAN'S DAUGHTER AND THE GENTLEMAN

THE MERRY MISFITS OF BATH ~ BOOK TWO

CALLIE HUTTON

Author's website: http://calliehutton.com/

Cover design by Maria Connor, My Author Concierge

Manufactured in the United States of America

First Edition December 2019

ABOUT THE BOOK

Must she pay for the sins of her mother?

Miss Charlotte Danvers has just received a life-altering shock. After spending most of her life in France in an elite school for girls, first as a student, and then as a teacher, she decides to return to London and take up residence with her mother.

When she arrives at her mother's townhouse in London, she is stunned to discover that the woman who raised her is the well-known courtesan, Mrs. Danforth.

After an angry and tearful confrontation with her mother, Charlotte leaves London and makes her home in Bath. All goes well until she meets Mr. Carter Westbrooke, close friend and business partner of Charlotte's best friend's husband, Lord Berkshire.

After only a few weeks, Mr. Westbrooke declares his intentions to Charlotte to make her his wife. She can be no gentleman's wife but cannot bring herself to tell him why. Must she run again?

To Maria, PA extraordinaire

PROLOGUE

London, England
November 1884

Miss Charlotte Danvers stepped out of the hackney she'd taken from the rail station to her mother's home right outside of Mayfair in London. She was excited at the surprise she planned for Mama.

Charlotte had spent most of her life in France at an exclusive girls' school. Once she graduated, with her mother's encouragement, she'd taken a teaching position at the school. That was three years ago, and now she was ready for the next phase in her life. The first step was moving to London to be with her mother.

She dropped the knocker on the front door as the hackney driver piled her luggage on the doorstep.

The door opened to an older man, obviously the butler, who stared at her as if he'd seen a ghost. "Miss Danvers? Surely that must be you."

"Yes!" She grinned. "I don't know who you are, but you seem to know me."

He bowed at her but looked a bit uncomfortable. "I would know you anywhere Miss Danvers. You look remarkedly like your mother."

"Yes. I've been told that many times." When the man continued to stare at her, she said, "May I come in?"

He stepped back, quite flustered. "Of course. My apologies, miss."

Charlotte drew off her gloves as she looked around the house she'd never seen before. Her earlier years had been spent in the country with a family who were friends of her mother. Mama told her she did not want her breathing in the putrid London air. Then at ten years of age, she'd been sent to the school in France.

"I hope my mother is home."

"Yes. She is. If you would retire to the drawing room, I shall inform her of your arrival."

Goodness, it all seemed so formal. What she wanted to do was race upstairs and find her mother and shout "surprise!" Wouldn't that bring a smile to her face?

Within minutes, the sound of footsteps rapidly coming down the stairs had Charlotte jumping up to meet her mother at the door to the drawing room. "Mama. Surprise! I left my position at the school and decided it was past the time I should join you here."

Mama looked quite pale under the makeup she wore. Charlotte had never seen makeup on her mother's face, so it was a surprise. She immediately decided she liked her better without face paint.

Her mother hugged her. "My dear. Yes, this is quite a surprise." She leaned back, her hands resting on Charlotte's shoulders and regarded her. "Why didn't you wire that you were coming?"

Charlotte grinned. "Then it wouldn't be a surprise,

would it?"

"No. Indeed it would not."

For the first time she could ever recall, Mama seemed to be at loss for words. "Are you well, Mama? Is something wrong?"

"Yes. No." She waved her arm around. "I am just trying to recover from this shock . . . rather, surprise."

"Yes. Isn't it wonderful? I decided it was time to start my life as a woman and maybe even look for a husband."

Mama drew a lace-edged handkerchief from the cuff of her dress and patted her face.

"You seem quite fancy," Charlotte said, "are you going out for the evening?"

"No. In fact, I am expecting some guests in a few minutes."

Charlotte clapped her hands. "Excellent! I shall love to meet some of your friends."

Mama paled even more and licked her lips. "My dear, as much as I would like you to meet my friends you do look quite peaked. I propose you retire to one of the bedchambers upstairs and enjoy a hot bath and some dinner, then a good night's sleep. We shall have a nice long chat in the morning over tea and one of Cook's famous breakfasts."

Although she did feel quite tired, she was disappointed that Mama didn't want her to meet her friends. "Perhaps you are right, Mama."

Her mother took a deep breath and let it out, her color returning somewhat. "I shall have Carlson—he is the man at the door—direct you to a lovely room that you can use. I'll then have Amy—my lady's maid—prepare a bath for you in the bathing room."

Mama hurried from the room, giving Charlotte time to look around. It was a well-appointed room in the taste she would expect from her mother. The furniture was elegant and well-made. The walls were papered with a pale green and rose stripes, with cream-colored wainscoting.

The man who met her at the door entered the room. "Miss, I had the footman bring your luggage up to the bedchamber Mrs. Danforth chose for your visit. If you will follow me, I will direct you there."

"Mrs. Danforth?"

The man looked confused. "Yes, Miss, that is the name your mother goes by."

"How very odd." There was no reason to inform the servant that this was no mere visit, but a permanent move to be with her mother. They'd been separated most of her life and now it was time for them to live together.

The bedchamber was as charming as all the other rooms she'd seen in the house. No surprise there, since Mama had excellent taste.

A middle-aged woman dressed in a maid's uniform greeted her as she entered the bedchamber. "Miss, your bath is ready. If you will follow me, I will show you where the bathing room is. I will be happy to unpack your things while you bathe."

"Thank you. Right now, all I need is in that small brown satchel. My nightgown, slippers, dressing gown, and other personal items are in there."

DESPITE HER LONG JOURNEY AND THE SOOTHING BATH AND wonderful dinner, Charlotte enjoyed in her room, she was still restless. Sleep would not come for hours, she was sure. She had a hard time accepting her mama's edict that she needed rest and should not meet her friends.

The sound of carriages drawing up to the house and then conversations from Mama's guests had been teasing her for a couple of hours. From what she could hear, the group seemed quite lively and free-spirited. Laughter erupted on occasion and someone played the piano.

Suddenly, she decided to dress in something simple and join the party. If she were going to begin her life as a woman, she must make decisions for herself. Hadn't she decided, without Mama's knowledge and consent, to leave her position at the school and join her mother in London?

Within minutes, she had shrugged out of her nightgown and dressed in a plain day dress since all her more formal gowns were hanging in the armoire horribly wrinkled from the trip.

With a quick glance in the mirror, she smoothed back her hair and left the room, excitement making her heart beat fast. This was her first party!

She didn't see Mama at first. There were about thirty guests, all dressed quite formally, which made her re-think her decision to come down dressed as plainly as she was.

A woman walked up to her, a glass of some sort of liquid in her hand. "I had no idea that Alice had a daughter, but you must be. You look exactly like her." Then she bent closer. "A much younger, version, though." She sipped her drink, winked at Charlotte, and walked off.

Whatever the woman said to two other women had them both turning her way, their eyebrows raised. Within minutes, she heard 'daughter' murmured among the crowd. She made a beeline to Mama, suddenly uncomfortable with the attention she was getting.

Not shy by nature, nevertheless, it seemed like her surprise to her mother was also a surprise to her friends. She felt a bit let-down that Mama had never told her friends that she had a daughter.

"Dearest, what are you doing here? I thought you were

asleep by now." Her mother's face had grown taut, revealing lines Charlotte hadn't noticed before. A gentleman walked up to Mama and touched her on the arm. "Is everything all right, my dear?"

He was an older man, very elegant and noble-looking. Even with his gray hair, he was a good-looking man with deep blue eyes and laugh crinkles at the corners. He eyed Mama with concern.

Mama smiled at the man. "Everything is fine, my lord."

She didn't introduce Charlotte to the man who seemed to be quite familiar with Mama. Truth be known, Charlotte had felt off-center since she'd arrived at Mama's house. By now she thought Mama would have gotten over her surprise arrival, but she seemed even more disconcerted than she had been earlier.

"I was too restless. I thought maybe spending some time down here with your friends would be nice." Charlotte mumbled the last part of her statement, aware of the gentleman next to Mama smiling at her.

Mama waved at a tall man in a livery, most likely a footman. "Please escort my daughter back to her room."

Charlotte's jaw dropped. Her mother was treating her like a child! "Thank you anyway, I shall find my own way." She glared at her mother. "Since I am not welcomed here." With a flounce of her skirt, she turned and strode toward the door. At the doorway, she turned back to see the gentleman and Mama in deep conversation.

She was almost to the staircase when a man called, "Wait."

Charlotte turned to see a young man, quite handsome actually, approaching her. He offered a slight bow. "I had no idea that Alice had a daughter. You are stunningly beautiful, like your mother."

"Thank you." Never comfortable with praise about her

looks, Charlotte dipped slightly and put her foot on the first step.

"May I speak with you a moment?" He reached out and touched her hand, which caused her to shudder. The man looked at her in such a way that she felt dirty. He looked her up and down like he was buying horseflesh.

"I think not, sir. I have the beginnings of a megrim. If you will excuse me."

"I am sorry to hear that, Miss Danforth. I just wanted to ask when you might be accepting a protector?"

"I am Miss Danvers, not Danforth." After her automatic correction, she took a second look at him, replayed his words in her head. The expression on his face, his question about taking a protector, her mother's overreaction at her arrival earlier, and the sort of people who were Mama's 'friends' caused a horrible thought to take hold of her mind. "I have no idea what you're talking about." The words were barely above a whisper.

"Oh, come now, Miss Danvers. There can be no other reason why your mother suddenly decided to show you off. What I don't understand is why she dressed you so plainly. You need to make use of those curves. And the neckline is much too high."

Her heart beat so fast, the thumping so loud, that she barely heard her own words. "And for what reason would my mother be showing me off, sir?" She knew she shouldn't ask that question, but she suddenly had no control over herself.

He frowned. "To follow in her footsteps as a well-known courtesan, of course."

1

London
One year later

CHARLOTTE, WHO WAS NOW KNOWN AS LOTTIE TO HER FRIENDS in Bath, took a final look in the mirror, pleased with her appearance. She rarely dressed so formally since she didn't attend the Assemblies and other social events in Bath where she'd lived for the past year, preferring to keep to herself, always afraid someone would recognize her.

However, today was Addie Mallory's wedding day. She, Addie, and Pamela were the best of friends and met for tea every day in Addie's bookstore, Once Upon a Book. Recently, Addie met Lord Berkshire and his adorable son, Michael, a deaf child. When his lordship asked Addie to accompany him, Michael, and Michael's governess to London for the purpose of seeking help for his son, he and Addie were caught in a compromising situation forcing them to marry.

From what Lottie saw when they were together, though, a marriage between them didn't appear to be much of a hardship for either the bride or the groom. There was definite affection between them. Maybe even more than that.

Addie had asked Lottie and Pamela to be her bridesmaids. Pamela was happy to do it, but Lottie had declined and thankfully Addie didn't question her further. They were both aware that Lottie had some sort of history in London and since that is where the wedding was taking place, Lottie preferred to stay in the background.

She was confident that her deep blue gown with the modest neckline, long sleeves, and loose-fitting skirt would not attract any unwanted attention. The guest list was quite small, and she hoped no one on the list recognized her as Mrs. Danforth's daughter. The clear glass spectacles she'd had specially made changed her appearance a bit.

Lottie slid a pearl-studded pin into her wide-brimmed straw hat, with the lovely blue flowers that matched her gown, to anchor it to her head. She glanced out the window, thankful that there were only a few clouds in the sky, so she needn't worry about rain ruining her outfit.

Satisfied with her appearance, she left the room she'd been given in the Mallory townhouse in Grosvenor Square. She knocked lightly on the door to Pamela's room. She opened the door and, as always, Lottie broke into a smile at her friend's current dilemma.

Pamela had a terrible stutter that only grew worse when she was flustered—as she was now—or when she met new people—which she was about to do. Pamela's dress was buttoned incorrectly, leaving the hem sort of on an angle. Her chignon was not doing a very good job of keeping her blond curls out of her face.

She took one look at Lottie and burst into laughter. "I k-know I'm a m-m-mess." She held her arms out to display the disaster.

"Here, let me help you." Lottie quickly refastened Pamela's gown and did her best to smooth back her curls. "Have you any more hairpins?"

Pamela nodded and hurried across the room to her satchel withdrawing a small box that she held out to Lottie. "Here."

Within minutes, Lottie had Pamela looking well put together. They linked arms and walked down the corridor to Addie's room.

"Oh my, you look beautiful," Lottie gushed as she and Pamela burst into Addie's room.

"I look like a bride." Addie smirked. "Something none of us ever planned on."

When the ladies first became friends, they assured each other that they were finished with the husband hunt. Though unusual, they were happy to make their own way as single women living on their own and providing their own income. It was quite freeing.

Lottie had not had the benefit of suitors or a 'husband hunt' since her unexpected arrival at her mother's house, and her subsequent quick move to Bath, squelched any idea Mama had for finding her a husband.

"Yes. And that is what you are," Lottie said in answer to Addie's statement. "Who would ever have guessed when Lord Berkshire walked into your bookstore the morning I was there to pick up my books, that he would end up your husband?" Lottie shook her head.

"I am sure stranger things have been recorded throughout time." Addie adjusted the top of her veil with a ring of fresh flowers that Addie's mother must have had a devil of a time finding at this time of the year.

"Adeline, it's time to leave for the church, dear." Mrs. Mallory entered Addie's room, studying her hands as she pulled on her gloves. She looked up and came to an abrupt halt. The woman's eyes filled with tears and she raised her hand to her mouth. "Oh, my."

Lottie felt her own eyes tear up, thinking of her mama, who, while she had certainly not forgiven her, she still missed something dreadful. She longed for her mother in little ways every day. Every time she smelled roses or fresh baked cookies like she and Mama used to eat in the bakery near school. Even though Lottie had spent all those years in France in a private boarding school, Mama had made the strenuous trip to visit her at least twice a month. They would stay in a fine hotel, eat decadent meals, and shop for ribbons, hats, perfumes, and jewelry. They saw the shows and visited the museums and laughed a great deal.

Unable to bear any more hugs and kisses between Addie and her mother, Lottie swiped at her eyes. "Enough of this," she said, waving her hand around. "I believe it is time for the church."

The four women made their way downstairs where Addie's father, Mr. Mallory, and brother, Marcus, waited to escort the ladies to the church.

"What a bevy of beauties," Marcus said as he made his bow to the ladies.

Lottie immediately froze at the man's words. A quick look in his direction assured her that he was not looking directly at her, but at his sister. Lottie let out the breath she'd been holding. She'd been nervous when she and Pamela had first been introduced to the young Mr. Mallory, but he didn't seem to know her, much to her relief.

She would be happy when this wedding was over, and she and Pamela were on the rail back to Bath.

They all trooped down to the two carriages to carry them to the church. Lord Berkshire had loaned one of his rented carriages so they could all travel at the same time to St. Paul's Cathedral where the wedding would take place.

THE TIME PASSED QUICKLY, AND THE CEREMONY WAS LOVELY. Lottie tried very hard not to wish for things she would never have. She was truly happy for her friend and was looking forward to helping her out by minding her store while she took her wedding trip and dealt with a legal problem involving her new stepson.

Lottie and Pamela had been taking turns running Addie's bookstore while Addie had been in London with Lord Berkshire. Lottie managed to take several shifts in addition to the work she did teaching young girls every week on the finer parts of being a lady. She tried not to laugh every time she thought of that term and how fast her student's parents would pull their daughters out of her lessons if they ever found out about her mother. They wouldn't be able to get their daughters far enough away from her.

But Lottie's years of training at the exclusive school she attended in France gave her the knowledge and confidence to take young girls under her wing and teach them dance, manners, watercolors, polite conversation, embroidery, and all the other things their parents wanted them to know before they were launched into Society.

The attendees at the wedding ceremony were joined by about fifty other guests for the wedding breakfast at Mr. and Mrs. Mallory's townhouse. Lottie was seated between Lord Berkshire's elderly uncle, Mr. Filbert, and the man who acted as witness for Lord Berkshire, his friend and business partner, Mr. Carter Westbrooke.

Mr. Filbert was slightly deaf and charming, trying his best to keep up a conversation even though she suspected he missed just about every other word. On the other hand, Mr. Westbrooke made her extremely nervous.

He was young, not deaf, but unquestionably charming. And quite handsome. His black as night wavy hair fell in loose curls around his head. As startling as his hair was, his blue eyes were of a shade so deep she had not seen it before.

Mr. Westbrooke was the sort of man who gave his entire attention to the person he was speaking with, making them feel as if they were the most important person in the room. His eyes were riveted on her face when he looked at her, and she felt as though he looked at her far too much.

He was dressed quite fashionably in charcoal gray trousers, a silver and blue waistcoat with a crisp white shirt, black ascot tie, and a fine wool jacket in black.

"So, Miss Danvers, the new Lady Berkshire tells me you have been friends with her ever since she moved to Bath."

"Yes." She picked up her fork and continued to eat, staring at her plate. If any of her students saw her, they would be aghast. She gave several lectures on polite conversation at balls, dinner parties, and other social events. Every rule she gave them was slowly but surely being broken by their teacher.

"Do you live with your family in Bath?" Mr. Westbrooke took a sip of his wine and continued to look in her direction.

Be polite. This is your best friend's wedding.

"No." She wished the blasted wedding breakfast over. So far no one had approached her to see if she was Mrs. Danforth's daughter. In fact, no one even gave her more than a glance. Except for Mr. Westbrooke.

The man in question was apparently not daunted by her abrupt—and very impolite—answer. He continued, "I don't remember seeing you about town."

She sucked in a breath in horror. "Do you live in Bath, Mr. Westbrooke?"

Please say no.

"I do. I have a legal practice in Bath where I run my various businesses as well. Lord Berkshire and I are long-time friends. We attended Harrow together."

"How very nice."

Blast it.

Avoiding men had been her strategy from the time she had fled London and made her home in Bath. She did not want to have anything to do with someone who might have spent time in her mother's bed. Just the thought made her stomach cramp. Since she had no way of knowing who Mama's clients had been over the years, it was best to avoid all men.

"Lady Berkshire also said you and Lady Pamela, have been running her store since she's been in London. That is quite nice of you."

It appeared Addie had done quite a bit of chatting about her and Pamela to this man. "I would do anything for Addie." She hesitated. "I apologize, I mean Lady Berkshire."

Mr. Westbrooke laughed and took another sip of wine. She decided at that point that his smile should be illegal. "You need not apologize to me. I'm sure no one would be surprised to hear you refer to your close friend by her first name."

"Nevertheless, it is poor manners and not the correct thing to do."

He leaned in close, causing her to move back. "Do you always do the correct thing, Miss Danvers?"

She did not want this man's attention. She wanted *no* man's attention. They were always after one thing. That one thing had destroyed her mother's life and consequently her life as well.

"Please excuse me." She stood abruptly, knocking her glass

of wine onto his leg. One look at his surprised expression and she turned on her heel and left the room.

CARTER JUMPED BACK AS THE CONTENTS FROM MISS DANVERS' glass of wine hit his thigh, the glass bouncing off and landing at his feet. The liquid—thankfully a white wine—splashed a bit onto his waistcoat as well, but not too much damage had been done, for which he was grateful, since he and a change of clothes were in different locations. Luckily, Miss Danvers had consumed most of her wine. He reached out and accepted a napkin from the footman's hand.

"My goodness, Mr. Westbrooke, what happened?" His hostess, the new Lady Berkshire viewed him with concern.

"Nothing to trouble yourself over, my lady. Miss Danvers merely had an accident with the wine." He blotted the liquid, hoping it would dry before the meal ended.

Lady Berkshire moved to stand, but her husband placed his hand over hers. "I think Miss Danvers is fine." He glanced over at Carter, a slight nod telling him he'd witnessed the mishap.

With everyone resuming their meal, Carter considered what had just occurred. Miss Danvers had looked both terrified and repulsed when she scrambled from her seat and made her quick exit. He felt the need to follow her and assure her whatever he'd said that caused her to run like that was meant in jest and he had no intention of harming her or seducing her.

Truthfully that last part wasn't quite accurate. Even with the spectacles, Miss Danvers was the most beautiful woman he'd ever seen. And he'd seen, danced with, conversed with, and slept with, enough of the fairer sex to make such a statement. He would not be a healthy young man if he didn't like the idea of bedding her.

She fascinated him. He'd been watching her since she'd caught his eye as she arrived at the church with Lady Pamela and the Mallory family. She was skittish, and nervous around him, but seemed quite relaxed when conversing with Lady Pamela and Lady Berkshire. She had remained with the receiving line once they'd entered the house, chatting with her friends, giving Carter an opportunity to study her further.

For a woman with such beauty, she did not seem at all vain or self-centered, which he'd seen in so many women who had more than average looks. In fact, given her dress for the occasion, it was almost as if she was trying to downplay her unusual countenance.

Odd, that.

Carter glanced at Miss Danvers' plate which still had quite a bit of food on it. He hated to think he caused her to miss her meal. He argued with himself and then finally, wet trousers or not, he pushed his chair back and stood. "Please excuse me for a moment," he said to the lady on the other side of him.

Perhaps what he was doing was foolish, but nevertheless something he felt he needed to do. A quick search of the house brought him to the drawing room where Miss Danvers stood, gazing out the window, a peaceful look on her face. So very different than she'd appeared when she had hurried off.

In order not to startle her, Carter cleared his throat. When she turned, he said, "I hope whatever it was I said didn't chase you from the celebration for your friend's nuptials."

She didn't appear quite as jumpy, and that encouraged him to slowly enter the room.

"I apologize if I alarmed or upset you in any way. That was certainly not my intent." He was mesmerized by her deep brown eyes and delicate demeanor. He wanted more than anything to wrap his arms around her and assure her he would never allow any harm to come to her.

She offered him a slight smile. "And I apologize for drenching you with my wine. It *was* accidental, you know."

He grinned, pleased to see she didn't move back as he approached her. "I believe you. I see no reason why you would purposely want to douse someone you just met with wine, unless he was truly offensive."

"No. That was not the case." She turned back to look out the window again.

"You left quite a bit of food on your plate. If you don't return, I shall feel guilty all day for denying you sustenance."

That brought a delightful laugh from her. The sound flowed over him like warm water: comforting yet enticing. Then she said, "I hardly think missing one meal will see me wither away."

He held out his hand. "Please. I will feel much better if you rejoined the party. I believe Berkshire and his bride are getting close to cutting that delicious looking wedding cake, and I do not want to miss the opportunity to assuage my sweet tooth."

She ignored his hand and moved around him, giving herself a wide berth. "In that case, I must return." She glanced back over her shoulder and smiled, stopping him dead in his tracks, his jaw slack. "You see, I have my own sweet tooth to satisfy."

Carter followed behind her like a puppy panting after its mistress. He had never in his entire life reacted this way to a woman. He knew deep inside it was not just her beauty, but her vulnerable demeanor and the sense of sadness that surrounded her. She'd been deeply wounded, and if it had been another gentleman to cause her such pain, he would find the man and teach him a lesson in behavior toward women.

Especially *this* woman.

"Is everything all right, Lottie?" Lady Berkshire glanced at the two of them as they arrived together. Hopefully, being alone with him for a few minutes would not cause a problem for Miss Danvers. The last thing he wanted was to endanger her reputation.

Carter pulled out Miss Danvers' chair. He eyed her plate with the now cold food and waved a footman over. "Please bring Miss Danvers hot food."

The man whipped away the plate, bowed, and left.

Miss Danvers shook her head. "That wasn't necessary. I had enough to eat."

"No. You didn't, and I don't wish to be subjected to you swooning because of a lack of nourishment."

She lifted her adorable little nose in the air. "I do not swoon."

"Never?" His brows rose.

"Never. A proper young lady keeps control of herself at all times."

Carter's eyes grew wide. "You sound like a teacher or a governess. Have I guessed correctly?"

"You are quite clever, Mr. Westbrooke. In fact, I am employed to prepare a group of young ladies who will shortly make their debut into Society."

Another footman appeared with a new glass for Miss Danvers and then proceeded to pour wine for them both. Carter raised his glass. "Here is to wine that lands in one's stomach, and not one's person."

Miss Danvers offered that mesmerizing smile again and lifted her glass. "Here is to women who accidentally upend their wine onto gentlemen who do not return the favor." After taking a sip, she said, "You don't intend revenge, do you?"

2

LOTTIE COULD NOT BELIEVE SHE WAS FLIRTING WITH MR. Westbrooke. She never had the chance to flirt, but she assumed that was what she was doing. She hated to admit something about the man charmed her. And it felt quite good, actually. She had behaved foolishly in jumping from the table and running off like a skittish colt. Quite childish, in fact, and somewhat disastrous for Mr. Westbrooke's trousers.

When she finally calmed down, she realized if he knew who her mother was, he would have said so immediately. That was not the type of thing a man kept to himself if he hoped to entice a courtesan's daughter into his bed.

She had the feeling that Mr. Westbrooke was honorable. A gentleman, whether by birth or behavior it didn't matter. She had acted like a lady her whole life, but she certainly wasn't one by birth.

Far from it, as she had learned.

"Thank you," Lottie said to the footman who placed a plate of food in front of her. She truly was no longer hungry: the little bit she'd eaten having satisfied her appetite. But considering the trouble Mr. Westbrooke had gone through, and the guilt for chasing her from her meal to which he had professed, she picked up her fork and gave it a try.

"I find I am fascinated by your employment." His easy smile did unfamiliar things to her insides. Nice, unfamiliar things. A spicy scent emanated from him that was pleasing to her senses, and his eyes held her captive. She could be in quite a bit of trouble with this man. Hopefully, this breakfast would be the only time she spent with him.

"Are you one of the Upper Ten Thousand yourself?"

That question took her by surprise and proved he did not know her. He might know her mother, but he hadn't made the connection, which was a possibility since she resembled her mother so much. She breathed a sigh of relief. "No," she laughed. "Not at all, but I was educated in a private boarding school for young ladies in France."

"Miss Danvers, you grow more interesting by the minute." He viewed her over the rim of his glass.

Lottie shook her head and placed her fork and knife on the plate to signal she was finished. She really did need to leave some space for that delicious looking cake. "I am hardly interesting, Mr. Westbrooke."

"I disagree. I think you are extremely interesting."

Just then Lord Berkshire rose and addressed the group. "My friends, my lovely new wife tells me it is time for us to cut the wedding cake." Cheers followed his announcement. Obviously, Lottie and Mr. Westbrooke were not the only ones interested in the sweets.

"Here, here," Mr. Westbrooke shouted, holding up his glass of wine.

"Only one piece for you, Carter," Lord Berkshire said. He turned to Addie and said *sotto voce,* "He would eat the entire thing if we let him."

Addie and Lord Berkshire each cut a small piece then the

cake was whisked off to the kitchen where it would be cut into helpings for the guests. Mr. Westbrooke's attention had been taken up by Lady Pemberton, the woman on his other side who was a friend of Mrs. Mallory's, which left Lottie attempting once again to converse with Mr. Filbert.

She had noticed Addie and her new stepson, who sat on the other side of his father, communicating by moving their hands, which she found fascinating. Addie had told her and Pamela about the method called sign language that Lord Berkshire had learned about and how it had helped his son. She wondered what it would be like for a young lady about to make her debut if she were deaf. It crossed her mind that a school to teach sign language to the hard of hearing, whether from birth or old age, would be quite beneficial in Bath.

The cake had been served, along with steaming pots of tea. By the time the meal had ended, Lottie felt the need for a nice long walk. She moved her chair back. "Please excuse me," she mumbled to Mr. Filbert and Mr. Westbrooke.

Mr. Westbrooke immediately stood. "Are you off to Bath today, Miss Danvers?"

"No. Lady Pamela and I are staying one more day and then we will take the rail back to Bath tomorrow."

"Excellent!"

She viewed him warily.

He took her arm and moved her forward. "I say that because I am staying at Lord Berkshire's home tonight and will return to Bath myself by rail in the morning."

She could no longer tell herself he had no interest in her. While it was not something she planned to encourage, it was rather nice to have the attention of a man for a short while. Especially a man as charming and handsome as Mr. Westbrooke.

Then he confirmed his interest. "Would you care for a

stroll before you retire to your bedchamber? I think all that food would digest better after a walk."

She hesitated then decided to enjoy herself for once instead of constantly hiding from everything. "Thank you, Mr. Westbrooke. I think a walk is an excellent idea."

She took his arm, and they strolled the area around the Mallory townhouse. The air was crisp and clean and raised her spirits considerably.

"Do you attend the Assemblies in Bath, Miss Danvers?"

"No." She shook her head. "I never seem to have the time." She didn't want to add that it was unseemly for a young woman to attend the Assemblies unescorted. But she feared the response that comment would bring from Mr. Westbrooke.

When she first arrived in Bath, she had the horrible feeling that everyone—especially men—who looked at her saw her mother. After a few months of practically hiding, she slowly eased her way into a somewhat normal life with her friends and her students. One that she enjoyed very much.

"Ah, so you tutor your young charges on Saturday evenings?" His smirk told her he didn't believe for one minute that she didn't have the time to attend a dance or two.

"Mr. Westbrooke!" She placed her hand on her chest. "Surely you are not calling me a liar?" She hoped her grin told him she was—dare she say it—flirting with him again. It felt rather nice, actually.

He bowed. "I would never do so, Miss Danvers. Let us just say I am questioning your memory. Does that suffice?"

As much as she was enjoying herself, she knew once she returned to Bath, she would resume the life she'd made for herself. This meant very little in the way of public events. Mr. Westbrooke was nice, and she rather enjoyed his company, but nothing could ever come of it.

With her background that she held close to her chest, she was not exactly marriage-worthy.

ONCE AGAIN, CARTER CHECKED THE NOTE HE'D RECEIVED FROM Berkshire confirming what time Lady Pamela and Miss Danvers were taking the rail back to Bath. He thoroughly enjoyed the stroll with Miss Danvers after the wedding breakfast, but when he pressed her as to when she was leaving the next morning, she'd withdrawn and became evasive about it. This had left him wondering if he'd done something wrong.

He picked up his satchel and headed for the front door. Berkshire and his bride were traveling to Brighton Beach for a short wedding trip. Carter had wished them a safe journey before he retired for the night. Then spent the next few hours tossing and turning and thinking about the beautiful woman with the deep brown eyes and sad demeanor.

It was a cloudy day, typical cool weather for London in November. He shrugged into his overcoat and made his way down the stairs to the waiting hackney. Traffic, as always, was heavy, but he arrived at Paddington Station in plenty of time for the rail to Bath. Since it was mid-morning, the flow of passengers was not as burdensome as earlier or later in the day.

There were enough people, however, to make searching for Miss Danvers and Lady Pamela difficult. Nevertheless, he strolled around and eventually just as the rail pulled into the station, he spotted the two women.

He purposely stayed back and watched them as they supervised the loading of their luggage onto the train, then mounted the stairs. He quickly handed his satchel to a porter and followed them up.

He was in luck because they took a double seat facing

another double seat which he commandeered before anyone else could grab it. "Good morning, ladies." He removed his hat and placed it on the seat alongside him to discourage any potential seatmates. He certainly did not want another man staring at Miss Danvers the entire trip.

"G-g-good morning, Mr. Westbrooke," Lady Pamela said, her face lighting up with pleasure.

He turned toward Miss Danvers. "How are you today, Miss Danvers?"

"Fine. Thank you." She turned and looked out the window, but before she did, he'd seen a bit of a smile on her face.

It appeared they were back to one-word answers. Well, he had a few hours to work his magic on the lady. He'd never had a problem before wooing a woman he was interested in. However, most of those efforts were spent on seduction. This time he was faced with a lovely young virtuous miss. The game was the same, the outcome different.

Although he wasn't certain what outcome he was anticipating, he had a good idea what direction he was headed with Miss Danvers.

TWO DAYS AFTER RETURNING FROM ADDIE'S WEDDING, LOTTIE sat at the back of Once Upon a Book going over the ledger. It appeared Addie's word blindness also carried over into her math ability. She had reversed several numbers, which Lottie fixed.

She really did enjoy helping in the store. At first, she'd been nervous thinking every man who walked into the place would know her, but eventually she calmed down and began to enjoy the work.

In fact, after a year in Bath, she'd begun to feel safe. The trip to London hadn't ended in the catastrophe she had feared. The entire time she fought the inclination to visit Mama. Then she remembered how her mother had deceived her, her whole life, and the feeling vanished.

She smiled as she remembered the trip back to Bath on the rail. Mr. Westbrooke was so charming that Pamela's stutter lessened, which didn't happen very often.

He had teased, cajoled, and flattered until Lottie gave in and allowed herself to enjoy his company. He told them interesting stories of his travels as a young man fresh out of University. She hung on his every word, seeing the exotic places through his eyes. Aside from her time in France—which had been spent behind the high brick walls of her school—she hadn't been anywhere.

Even though he'd showered them with attention, it was obvious his main interest lay with her. Even Pamela mentioned it when they parted ways at the rail station.

"It appears y-you have a s-suitor, Lottie," Pamela said as they settled into the hackney to return to their respective homes.

"No. I do not have a suitor. Mr. Westbrooke was just being charming and making the long trip to Bath more pleasurable."

Pamela laughed. "I don't t-think so. He was n-nice to both of us, b-but he looked at y-you in a special way.

Lottie waved her off but couldn't lie to herself. Mr. Westbrooke had indeed shown her more attention than Pamela, and the special way Pamela said he watched her made her insides tingle.

She closed both the ledger book and the thoughts that were teasing her mind. She stood and stretched, looking around the store. She loved books as much as Addie did. When things were slow, she allowed herself to wander the shelves and pick out a book to read that interested her. It had been pouring outside since she'd opened the store earlier, so chances were this would be a very slow day.

She was so captivated by Mark Twain's *The Adventures of Huckleberry Finn*, that she actually jumped when the front door opened and the little bell hanging over the door rang. She glanced up to see Mr. Westbrooke walking toward her. "Good day, Miss Danvers."

Lottie slammed the book shut and stood. "Good day to you as well, Mr. Westbrooke. Whatever brings you out in this terrible weather?"

He slid his wet umbrella into the umbrella stand by the door. "I had the urge to buy a new book."

The twinkle in his eyes told her that was not the absolute truth, but she preferred to ignore that. She also valiantly tried to disregard her racing heart, the tingle low in her stomach, and her suddenly dry mouth. "Well, since you are so hungry for a new book, we have many." She waved her arm around and banged her hand into one of the shelves. "Ouch."

"Are you all right?" He hurried to her side.

For goodness sake, she was nothing but a bumbling idiot around this man. Besides the wine she'd dumped onto his lap at the wedding breakfast, she also tripped over who knew what during their stroll, then stumbled into his arms alighting from the rail when they returned from London. She'd been quite annoyed with herself on how much she enjoyed his strong arms wrapping around her and the scent of tangy outdoors that emanated from his person.

She nodded. "Yes. Quite." She surreptitiously rubbed her hand. "Do take your time and browse."

He bowed. "Thank you. I will do that."

Lottie returned to her book, but no longer did it hold her attention. She was too riveted by the man pulling out a book, flipping through the pages, returning it to the shelf, and repeating the action several times over. His time was spent in the history area of the bookstore.

Why didn't he say something to her? The silence was killing her. She did not believe for one minute that Mr. Westbrooke was so in need of a book to read—since most gentlemen had their own libraries—that he came out in the pouring rain to find one. And then chose this bookstore among all the others in Bath.

Had Pamela been correct, and he was interested in her as a suitor? The initial jolt of excitement was quickly quelled by her common sense telling her that probably was not so, and even if it were, she had no intention of getting involved with a man. That led to courtship and eventually a proposal of marriage.

Unfortunately, not something she could consider.

Back to *The Adventures of Huckleberry Finn.* With determination, she returned to her book and read about three sentences before she looked up at Mr. Westbrooke again. His damp-from-the-rain hair was curled over his collar in the back of his head and skimmed his forehead. She had the urge to run her fingers through the silky black strands and push them back. Except they would probably just fall back again. Was she to stand there all day pushing his hair back? She giggled.

He looked up.

She looked back at her book, her face flushed.

Peeking at Mr. Westbrooke from underneath her eyelashes, the side view she had of him was impressive. Strong chin, full lips, aristocratic nose—somewhere in his ancestry there had been nobility—and a casual stance, with one knee bent as he flipped through the pages of the tome he held. Were he not wearing an Inverness cape she would also see his muscular thighs, broad shoulders, and trim waist.

Not that she'd noticed any of that during the wedding

breakfast.

She returned to her book. One full paragraph. She looked up again. Why was he not speaking to her?

He turned toward her, and she quickly looked down at her book, knowing another blush was climbing up her face. She studied him from under her lashes to see him grinning in her direction. The devil take it, he'd caught her watching him.

She closed the book and stood. It was not proper for her to be reading while there was a customer in the store, anyway. She strode, quite purposefully, to the front of the store and pulled out the feather duster from under the counter. Humming nothing in particular, she tackled the first book-case; dusting enthusiastically, even though she'd performed that task earlier.

"This seems like a good book."

Lottie jumped at the sound of Mr. Westbrooke's voice so close to her. She drew in a sharp breath to see him standing not more than three feet from where she dusted. "Excuse me?"

He held up *The Archipelago on Fire* by Mr. Jules Verne. "Have you read it?"

Her tongue caught in a tangle, she could only shake her head. Why was he standing so close that she could smell his bath soap? It was time to take control. After all, she was an employee. Or a substitute. Or a friend of the owner. Or all three. "No. I have not read that book." She backed away to make her escape and crashed into the bookcase behind her. Four books fell to the floor. When she bent to retried them, so did Mr. Westbrooke and they knocked heads.

"Ouch." She rubbed her head and dropped the book she had picked up. Feeling like a fool, she said, "I apologize, Mr. Westbrooke. It seems it is not healthy for you to be around me. I dread to think what mishap I will bring about next. Your very life could be in danger."

3

If Carter hadn't been so happy to see the effect he was having on Miss Danvers, he would feel sorry for her. She was truly at sixes and sevens since he'd arrived. That was a good sign. He much preferred that to apathy. The rail ride home had been pleasant with him keeping the ladies entertained. He had also brought a lunch basket with him, compliments of Ross & Hager, a fine restaurant he patronized whenever in London.

They shared pâté, cheese, fruit, crackers, cold chicken, and apple tarts, along with lemonade. He thought he'd made progress in his courtship of Miss Danvers. Especially when she stumbled from the steps leaving the rail car and landed very nicely in his arms, all warm and soft and womanly. The surprise on her face when she looked up at him had soon turned to something else as they stared briefly at each other.

However, when they parted at the rail station, she thanked him for the meal and quickly linked her arm in Lady Pamela's and practically dragged her to the hackney he'd hired for the two ladies, leaving him no chance for a private word with her.

Not to be deterred, he made the trip today in the pouring

rain because he had to see her again. The day before had been taken up with business he needed to attend to for himself and Berkshire while the man was on his wedding trip.

"Is there anything else I can help you with, Mr. Westbrooke?" Miss Danvers said.

Ah, if only you could read minds, Miss Danvers. You would know precisely how you can help me.

Carter offered her one of his best smiles. One that generally got a lady to agree to just about anything he proposed. "Can I get you to call me Carter? I feel we are friends enough for that allowance."

He barely got the words out before Miss Danvers shook her head. "No. I don't believe that is proper. We only just met."

"I see," he said, cupping his chin with his index finger and thumb. "How long do we need to know each other for that to occur? Or does it depend instead on how many times we are together? Or perhaps on whether we are in a crowd, or alone?"

She was just beginning to grin when the door to the store opened, the little bell ringing, announcing the presence of someone to interrupt his conversation.

He did not imagine the breath of relief Miss Danvers blew out as she said, "Excuse me." She skirted around him and hurried over to the young woman with a small child clinging to her skirts. What mother brought her young child out in this rain? Especially when he was making progress with Miss Danvers, he groused.

He resumed browsing the shelves. He did truly want to buy a book since he spent most of his leisure time reading. A perfect evening for him would be a small glass of brandy or port at his side as he sat in front of his fireplace reading a good book. He oftentimes imagined a wife sitting there alongside him, doing her embroidery or reading, as well. Then when the night grew late, they would hold hands as they climbed the stairs together and spend time in bed making love.

He had always intended to marry, but at thirty years of age, he'd never met anyone with whom he felt he could share the rest of his life. He attended the dances at the Bath Assembly Rooms on occasion and knew many of the single women in the town. At least those who were on the hunt for a husband.

Despite his mother's insistence, he refused to enter the London Marriage Mart fray. The mothers there were downright scary. His brother, Charles, had been caught in a noose by a young lady who he accidentally compromised. Luckily for him, Lady Hastings turned out to be not such a bad wife.

Since he'd never seen Miss Danvers, either at London society events or the Bath Assembly, and had not met her at any other social event in the past year she had lived in Bath, he assumed she was not interested in a husband. It was quite preposterous to assume that a beauty like her would not have men dropping proposals at her feet left and right.

He returned the book he'd been looking through and glanced over at Miss Danvers, who was bending down speaking to the young child.

She had a way of speaking that mesmerized him. She was all hands and gestures when she spoke, even though he was quite certain the proper boarding school she had attended would have frowned upon that. What baffled him was why a woman as beautiful as Miss Danvers, along with her charming personality and kindness, was *not* searching for a husband.

There was no doubt in his mind that she'd been brought up a lady and her parents would expect her to make a successful match. If she didn't want a husband, he wanted to know why. He was almost certain she was suffering from a broken heart.

He managed to keep himself busy while Miss Danvers

dealt with the customer. After a lengthy discussion and a purchase of two children's books, the woman and her charge left the store.

"Miss Danvers, may I entice you to join me for lunch?" He glanced out the window, something he'd already done before he raised his question. "It appears the rain has stopped. If you will do me the honor of accepting my invitation, I can escort you in my carriage to whichever restaurant you fancy."

She hesitated, her teeth clamping down on her lovely lower lip. He wanted to cover those lips with his own and run his tongue over them until she opened, allowing him to taste her. Feel the velvet of her mouth, the softness of her tongue. "I am sure Lady Berkshire doesn't expect you to bypass lunch to take care of her store."

Miss Danvers shook her head. "No. In fact, when Lady Berkshire was in town, she, Lady Pamela, and I met every day here in the store for a late lunch, or I guess you could call it tea. But Lady Pamela is unable to meet today since she has a new pupil and she needs more time to evaluate her music skills."

Lady Pamela had mentioned on the trip home from London that she taught piano, violin, and voice to young students. It amazed him that someone with her stutter could teach voice. But Miss Danvers had assured him that Lady Pamela sang like an angel.

"Then you are free for lunch." He didn't want to make that a question and give her a chance to find some excuse.

The indecision on her face was almost comical. It was as if he was asking her to run away to Gretna Green with him. "It's only lunch, Miss Danvers," he said softly.

She laughed. "I know that. I was just thinking about the propriety of it."

The woman was certainly overly concerned with propriety

as if she'd been raised in a convent or by a vicar, rather than a posh school for girls. He would love to delve further into her childhood to see what had made her the way she was.

"We will be in a public restaurant. It is daylight. There is nothing to be worried about. I guarantee you I am a gentleman."

She studied him for a minute, then said softly, "I believe you are."

Why that simple sentence brought such a jolt of happiness to him was disconcerting. Surely, he wasn't that taken with Miss Danvers.

She grinned and he almost lost his breath. Yes, he was that taken.

"If you are certain you are not concerned about risking your life considering my record with you so far, then very well. It will only take me a few minutes to put the closed sign on the door and fetch my coat and hat."

He fought the inclination to shout *hurrah!* As he'd pointed out to Miss Danvers, it was only lunch.

She sat very demurely across the seat from him in his carriage, her hands placed delicately in her lap. Despite his assurances that he was a gentleman, she still looked a bit nervous and continued to lick her lips as she gazed out the window. Every time he saw that sweet little pink tongue run around her lips his cock hardened. He'd never been attracted to the sweet, demure, fragile type of woman before, but this one had him twisted in knots.

Even though she was all sweetness and light, he had a strong feeling that she was steel underneath. To make her own way from London to Bath, and support herself, showed bravado rarely seen in a young lady.

"I told my driver to take us to Sally Lunn's House since you had no preference. I hope that meets with your approval?"

"I love Sally Lunn's buns." Lottie laughed. "I find the need to laugh every time I say that."

Her joy was contagious. "Yes. I agree. It is quite musical. And the buns are wonderful."

The carriage stopped in front of Sally Lunn's House on North Parade Passage, across from The Parade Gardens. Carter stepped out of the coach and turned to help Miss Danvers down. His large hand swamped her small, delicate one. He looked up at her as she took his hand and their eyes met. Her chocolate brown expressive eyes and the touch of her hand did something very strange to his insides.

Carter had never really thought much about love at first sight, believing it was something found in silly romance novels, but it was beginning to appear that not only was there such a thing, but it had happened to him.

Either that or he was coming down with an ague.

LOTTIE SHIVERED AS SHE TOOK MR. WESTBROOKE'S HAND in hers as he helped her from the carriage. He looked as startled as she felt, almost as if something unusual and rare had passed between them. She needed to stop this nonsense. Anything more than friendship between her and Mr. Westbrooke was doomed from the start.

She was who she was, and he was . . . a man. She'd sworn on her tearful trip from London over a year ago that for her men and marriage was a crushed dream. If not happy, she'd at least been content with that certainty. Until . . .

Chastising herself, she focused her attention on the lovely restaurant. She'd always loved Sally Lunn's buns and enjoyed the history behind one of the oldest buildings in Bath. According to the current owners of the bakery and restaurant, the building was erected in 1482, and the famous Sally Lunn began baking her buns there in 1680.

They were seated in the main dining room which was a beautifully decorated space. The walls were painted a pale yellow, which along with the wide windows in the front of the building gave the space a great deal of light. In the decorating, they had kept the essence of the age of the building. Drawings and paintings along the walls of the original kitchen with Sally Lunn doing her baking were fascinating.

"I love this tea shop. If I could, I would have one of these buns every day, but I'm afraid in no time at all my dresses would no longer fit." She smiled at Mr. Westbrooke as she picked up the menu the waiter had placed in front of them.

"I agree. This is one of my favorite spots, as well. It has so much history connected to it."

"Are you fond of history, then, Mr. Westbrooke?"

He studied her over the top of the menu. "Indeed. It is my favorite subject. I excelled in it at school."

Lottie stared at him open-mouthed. "How very odd. It was my favorite subject as well. I won awards every year for the school's history essay contest."

"Ah, yes. The private school for girls in France."

She smiled, warmed by the memories of her school. "Yes, it was located in a small town outside of Paris."

"Paris? I assume you are fluent in French?"

"*Absolument! C'est presque ma langue maternelle.*" She grinned.

"*Bien joué.*" He dipped his head and smiled back. "*Tu m'as convaincu.*"

Lottie hated the warmth that flowed through her at their bantering. They did truly have much in common. Their best friends were married to each other, they both loved history, and they both were fluent in French.

This is what she'd expected when she left France to take up what she thought would be a wonderful new life with Mama.

They studied the menu, then placed their order. Now that the preliminaries were out of the way, Lottie felt a bit more relaxed. Mr. Westbrooke possessed the skill and charm to make her feel at ease. Perhaps they could have a friendship of sorts after all since nothing more was possible.

"What made you move from London to Bath?" Mr. Westbrooke broke the silence with an awkward question.

She didn't like the idea of lying to him, but she was certainly not going to tell him the true story. "I found when I returned to London from France, I was not comfortable there." She shrugged. "So noisy, dirty, and smelly."

He nodded. "Another thing we agree upon. I only visit London when I absolutely must. Like a few times a year when my mother expects the family to assemble for holidays and, of course, her birthday." He studied her for a minute. "Do you miss your family?"

"I only have my mother." She scrambled to think of more to say. When she'd met Addie and Pamela, they accepted her story that she and her mother had a break in their relationship, and she left London. Too ashamed of her background when she first made their acquaintance to add to the story, she told them no more. Since then they accepted her friendship without further questions.

"I'm sorry," Mr. Westbrooke said. "When did you lose your father?"

I never had him to lose. He was probably someone passing through the night.

"I never knew him." There, the truth. Before he could continue with the questions, she jumped in, "And your family? Do you have siblings?"

The waiter placed dishes of shepherd's pie in front of each of them, along with a platter of jellied eels and kippers in the center of the table. Lottie scrunched up her nose.

"You don't care for eels?"

Lottie shook her head. "No. I definitely do not like jellied eels. Or kippers, either."

Mr. Westbrooke shook out his napkin and placed it on his lap. He picked up his fork and said, "To answer your question, I have two brothers, no sisters."

She always wanted a sister or even a brother. Just someone else she could share her childhood with who would always be in her life. "I am envious. I would have loved a sibling."

He laughed. "There were times when I would have packed them up and sent them off to France."

"Are you the eldest?" The shepherd's pie was delicious, and she almost found herself groaning with pleasure.

He shook his head. "No. My brother, Charles, Viscount Hastings, is the eldest. Then comes my brother, Peter, and then me." He continued to eat not realizing he just sucked all the air out of the room and turned her world completely upside down.

"Your brother is a viscount?" she said holding her fork between the plate and her mouth.

He shook his head. "In some ways. It is a courtesy title from my father, the Earl of Huntingdon."

Lottie lowered her fork and fought the nausea rising in her stomach. "Your father is an earl?"

"Yes. But I am a lowly Mr. Westbrooke." He shook his head and smiled. "Thank heavens. I would not want the responsibility and confinement of a title."

A loud buzzing began in her ears and Lottie felt as though his voice came from a distance. This man was a member of the *ton*. One of the Upper Ten Thousand. He came from nobility.

His blood was bluer than the ink she used for her correspondence. She pushed her food away.

"I say, Miss Danvers, are you all right? You seem to have gone quite pale."

She used all the training she'd had over the years on how to conduct oneself in polite company and offered a smile. "I am quite well. It turns out I am not as hungry as I thought."

He continued to study her. "Perhaps it's the sight of the eel and kippers. I can have the waiter remove them." He turned and signaled for the man to approach their table.

"Will you please take the platter way?"

"Tea." Lottie managed to get out. "I would like some tea. And I'm finished with my food."

"And please remove my companion's plate and bring tea." Mr. Westbrooke turned to her once the waiter left with the dishes piled in his arms. "I am sorry you've lost your appetite. I do believe it was the eels and kippers that did you in." He offered her a soft smile that made her want to cry.

He was such a nice man. So thoughtful and caring. Someone that she would have wanted to marry before her life changed forever. Although she didn't expect to become involved with a man, she had the feeling if things were different, Mr. Westbrooke would be someone she could care for.

Or even love.

She would not weep.

CARTER CONTINUED WITH HIS LUNCH BUT KEPT A CLOSE EYE ON Miss Danvers. Something had definitely upset her. The only thing he could think of was when he mentioned his brothers and father. Did she have some sort of dislike of the nobility? Had her heart been broken by a member of the *ton*? That would certainly explain why she left London to strike out on her own.

No matter what the reason was, the remainder of the lunch was stilted and uncomfortable. Miss Danvers didn't eat any of the tarts or biscuits that were placed on the table with the tea but did down two cups of the brew. She responded to all his questions with one-word answers until he began to feel as though their time together was turning into the Spanish Inquisition.

Reluctantly, he called for their bill, paid it and assisted her outside back to his carriage. The sun had peeked through the clouds while they were in the restaurant, which should have cheered him since he loved the sunshine, but he still had the let-down feeling of having lost Miss Danvers.

They said very little on the way back to the store. He helped her from the carriage and escorted her to the door. She took a ring of keys from her reticule and slid one of them into the lock. Before she opened the door, she turned to him. "Thank you for lunch."

"You are welcome, but I feel as though you really didn't enjoy yourself." He placed his knuckle under her chin and moved her head so he could look into her eyes. "What happened?"

She pulled back and began to fidget with her reticule. "Nothing. Everything was fine." She smiled, but the effort didn't reach her eyes. Her sad eyes.

"Then may I ask you to attend the Assembly with me this Saturday?"

She turned the knob and moved so quickly to enter the store that she almost fell over a small table with a display of books. He reached out and grabbed her and she quickly pulled away. "I am afraid I will be unable to attend." Her face was flushed, and she looked about to cry.

It was time to withdraw. Whatever had upset her continued to bother her and he seemed to be making things worse. "Very well. I am sorry you will not be able to attend."

When she said nothing in return, but looked away, waiting for him to leave, he gave her a short bow and said, "Thank you again for spending time with me, Miss Danvers. Have a pleasant day."

She nodded and he left the store.

Carter went over in his mind the entire time they were together and concluded that the lunch was truly a surreal experience. No matter how many times he considered their brief conversation, the only thing that stood out in his mind was when he said his father was an earl and his brother held his courtesy title of viscount.

Even if she'd had a bad experience with someone from the *ton*, her reaction to knowing about his family was excessive. However, not the sort to give up easily on something that had become important to him, he decided not to take her actions today as final. When he wanted something, he did not give up until it looked hopeless.

It was far too soon in their acquaintance for him to assume Miss Danvers had no interest in him. He'd known enough women to sense when there was interest, and Miss Danvers was not immune to him. He would retreat, give her some time, then forge his battle again.

4

As impatient as he was, Carter still managed to wait several days before again visiting the bookstore. However, he was disappointed to find Lady Pamela in charge and Miss Danvers nowhere in sight.

"G-g-good afternoon, Mr. W-w-westbrooke." Lady Pamela greeted him as he entered. He tried very hard not to show his disappointment since he didn't want to insult Lady Pamela.

"Good afternoon to you as well, Lady Pamela. You are looking quite well."

She blushed. "T-thank you."

He glanced around the store, then casually asked, "The last time I was here, Miss Danvers was in charge. Do you take turns?" Hopefully that question wasn't too blatant, but by the slight smile she offered him, he didn't think he'd fooled her.

"Yes, we d-do take t-turns. Her d-day is t-t-tomorrow." Although it was quite painful to listen to the poor girl, Carter allowed her to take her time to say what she wanted to say. Stuttering must be a very annoying affliction.

Trying to dispel the real reason for his visit, he nodded. "I will take a look around."

He browsed for about fifteen minutes finding two books he would add to his library, when the door opened, and Miss Danvers entered. His heart sped up and he chided himself for his foolishness.

She didn't see him at first, and to keep it that way, he moved behind a bookcase that blocked him from her view. She pulled off her gloves and having spotted Lady Pamela, moved toward her. "How is business?"

"Fine. We have been busy enough."

Carter was amazed at how easily Lady Pamela had responded to Miss Danvers. Apparently, her stutter was less prevalent when she was speaking to a friend. He wasn't overly familiar with the affliction, but that explanation made sense.

The two women put their heads together and Carter knew precisely when Lady Pamela told her he was in the store because Miss Danvers stiffened, and for a moment, he thought she would flee. Before she could do that, he stepped out from behind the bookcase. "Good afternoon, Miss Danvers."

"Mr. Westbrooke." she nodded at him. "Such a surprise." Her smirk baffled him. Was she pleasantly surprised, or annoyed?

"I am afraid w-w-e are about t-t-to close the store for our t-t-tea break," Lady Pamela said. He then noticed the store was empty except for the three of them. "W-w-would you c-c-care to join us f-for tea?"

Miss Danvers swung her eyes to Lady Pamela with an expression that should have set the poor woman's clothes on fire. The polite thing to do was refuse since it was obvious Miss Danvers did not want him there, but he could not let this opportunity pass him by.

Instead, he bowed. "I would be delighted to have tea with such charming ladies. Thank you very much."

· · ·

LOTTIE WANTED TO SHAKE PAMELA. THE LAST THING SHE wanted to do was sit down again with the earl's son. That was how she'd thought of him since their ill-fated lunch when she learned he was a member of the *ton*. He must surely know her mother. Or at least know about her. As she tossed and turned in bed that night, she had the horrible thought that perhaps he'd even availed himself of her services.

It was that consideration which sent her to the water closet to bring up the little bit of food she'd eaten that day. Then she calmed herself with the thought that if he knew her mother that well, he would have noticed—and most likely commented on—the likeness between them.

She had been much happier living in Bath dealing with her young charges and her two friends before Mr. Westbrooke had entered her life. Why couldn't he go away and leave her alone? Then she wouldn't have to acknowledge this ridiculous pull she had toward him.

As they made their way to the back of the store, Lottie fought the beginning of a megrim. She glanced at Mr. Westbrooke as they all settled in the chairs surrounding the table that held their tea things. He was still studying her in a way that only put her more on edge. He was such a wonderful man, she hated that he might think she didn't care for him.

She did care for him. Probably much more than she should. But she could not change who she was or who he was. His family no doubt expected him to make an excellent match and that certainly did not mean a courtesan's daughter. They would be appalled.

Pamela hopped up and retrieved another cup, saucer, and plate for their guest and began to pour the tea.

Lottie was afraid to even pick up her cup since she knew her hand was shaking like leaves clinging to the branches in a windstorm. If she were to get through this, she had to gain control of herself. She was a strong woman, and it was only tea.

She took a few breaths and looked Mr. Westbrooke in the eye. "I see you have two books there, Mr. Westbrooke. What have you selected today?" She congratulated herself. Despite the perspiration that had broken out on her upper lip and forehead, she managed to speak like a normal person.

She had actually put two sentences together and did not trip over her words or sound like a squeaking mouse. Nor had she dropped a biscuit in his lap, or dumped tea over his head.

The smile he bestowed on her alarmed her. It was apparent she'd made him happy by simply speaking with him.

Please, no. No, no, no.

He picked up the two books and looked at the covers. "*Flatland* by Edward Abbot Abbot." He grinned. "I don't know why he has two of the same names." He placed that book back down on the table and read the other one. "*A Little Tour of France* by Henry James."

"Oh, Mr. Westbrooke, d-d-did you know M-m-miss Danvers went to s-s-school in France?" Lady Pamela said.

"Yes. Miss Danvers shared that information with me."

"How very odd that you chose that book," Lottie said. It could have been a coincidence, but she didn't think so. "Just as strange as you popping up in Lottie's bookstore twice in the past week."

He had the decency to flush. "I've always had a great deal of interest in France, actually. And books." Mr. Westbrooke laid that book on top of the other one. "Now I have a question for you ladies."

Force of habit had Lottie sitting quite still, almost as if waiting for a blow.

"Y-yes, Mr. W-w-westbrooke?" Pamela sat forward; her pretty face full of curiosity.

"I would love to escort both of you lovely ladies to the Assembly Rooms Saturday evening."

"Oh, how lovely," Pamela said. She turned to Lottie. "Isn't that wonderful, Lottie? We've always wanted to go, but never had an escort."

"Yes. Just lovely." Lottie glared at Mr. Westbrooke who had the temerity to grin.

LOTTIE PACED HER SMALL BEDROOM THINKING OF EVERY EXCUSE she could possibly come up with to add to the partially written note, addressed to Mr. Westbrooke, sitting on her desk in the corner of the room.

Whatever had possessed her to agree to attend the Saturday Assembly with Mr. Westbrooke and Pamela? She'd purposefully avoided all social events since her arrival in Bath, except for the occasional trip to the theater with her friends.

She stared at the note and chewed her lower lip. Truthfully, she was so very tired of hiding. She was young and enjoyed all the things a young lady would enjoy. Theater, museums, Assembly dances, strolls in the park, dinner at a fancy restaurant. Perhaps she could never have a suitor since she wasn't fit for marriage, but she could certainly attend more events than an infrequent night at the theater.

The wedding in London had not resulted in disaster, so perhaps it was time to enjoy a bit of social life. Before she could change her mind, she tore the note into shreds and dropped it into the rubbish. Then dusted her hands off with determination and opened the door to her closet to select a gown for the evening.

She chose a deep green satin with black trim that she'd

worn to a ball in France. The bodice was a modest cut with a row of black lace edging. The fabric was snug against her waist and tummy and gathered in the back in a slight bustle.

Her black slippers that matched the lace on the gown were still in perfect shape, a reminder that she had attended that ball as a teacher and chaperone, so had not danced.

She managed to wrestle her dark brown curls into a simple topknot with a few strands resting on her neck and at the sides of her face. A sweet little matching green hat with black netting sat on top of her head, nothing more than a decoration.

Quite satisfied with how she looked, she picked up her cloak and waited in the parlor for Mr. Westbrooke to arrive.

Within minutes, she heard the sound of carriage wheels and then a slight knock on her front door. She opened the door and her breath caught. He looked dashing. Why did he have to be so charming and handsome?

He extended his elbow. "Are you ready, Miss Danvers?"

She contemplated chastising him for the way he'd maneuvered her into attending the Assembly by asking Pamela. But then decided to allow him this one sneaky ploy.

"Yes, Mr. Westbrooke. I am ready."

LOTTIE HAD TO ADMIT SHE WAS ENJOYING THE EXCITEMENT OF arriving at the Assembly Rooms. She'd never seen them before and was quite taken with the glimpse she'd gotten of lovely pale blue walls, white trim, and numerous chandeliers hanging from the ceiling. The room was three or four times the size of her entire flat.

They handed off their coats to a man stationed at the door, then taking a deep breath, Lottie took Mr. Westbrooke's arm.

He extended his other elbow to Pamela, and the three of them entered the room.

It was like a fairyland from a child's book. The women were all dressed in lovely evening gowns of various colors. Deep blue, red, green, and gold gowns flashed by as the dancers swayed and dipped to a waltz. Every sort of fabric was represented, too. Satin, silk, fur-lined collars of light wool gowns, and even a few velvets.

The gentlemen were as well turned out as the ladies. Dark trousers, stark white shirts, colorful waistcoats, and well-tied ascots, all covered with dark jackets. She watched the dancers for a while, noting none of the gentlemen were as handsome as Mr. Westbrooke.

He bent toward Lottie's ear, the warm scent of his bath soap tickling her nose. "I take it since you teach young ladies how to move about in Society that you are an excellent dancer."

Lottie loved to dance. In France, she had been allowed to attend a few events as a guest and not just a chaperone and enjoyed the dancing so much she even wore out a pair of slippers one time. "I don't know that I am an excellent dancer, but certainly an enthusiastic one."

"Ah. Modesty on top of all your other qualities." He grinned, the light from the chandeliers reflected in his eyes. Her heart took an extra beat and the smile she intended to give him faltered. She did not know what to make of the effect he was having on her.

The music ended and the dancers scattered from the middle of the floor. Some to join friends on the side, some to avail themselves of the refreshments at the long table on the south wall of the room.

"Westbrooke. Why is it you always end up with the most beautiful ladies in the room?" A tall, slender man slapped Mr.

Westbrooke on the back and stared at the two women, with a particular interest in Pamela. "Do I get an introduction?"

Mr. Westbrooke turned to her and Pamela. "Ladies, may I make known to you, Mr. Nicholas Smith." He gestured toward the man. "Smith, this is Lady Pamela and Miss Danvers."

They both gave a slight dip and Mr. Smith bowed. "I will certainly be happy to take one of these lovely ladies off your hands, Westbrooke." He turned to Pamela. "May I request a dance, Lady Pamela?"

"Y-y-yes. That w-would be f-f-ine." Pamela's blushed rose from the top of her bodice to her hairline. Yet, she was speaking to a stranger and agreeing to a dance. It seemed to Lottie that the two of them were facing their demons tonight.

She swore Mr. Westbrooke had tensed when Mr. Smith mentioned taking one of them off his hands and then visibly relaxed once he chose Pamela.

The four of them chatted about the usual things, England's weather, parliament's latest blunder and the horrible condition of the roads. Mr. Smith was a pleasant man, of average looks, but with the way of smiling that transformed his face into something much more attractive. And he seemed to be doing a great deal of smiling in Pamela's direction.

The Master of Ceremonies announced the next dance, a quadrille, which had Lottie already tapping her feet before the music even began.

"It appears you are anxious to join the others on the dance floor," Mr. Westbrooke said. He took Lottie's arm and moved them to the end of a line of dancers. Mr. Smith and Pamela were right behind them and took the positions next to them.

It was a lively dance, and Lottie was pleased to discover that Mr. Westbrooke was a wonderful dancer. The intricacies of the steps didn't allow for much conversation, but she found herself smiling quite a bit.

And Mr. Westbrooke smiling right back.

She took a deep breath as the number ended. "That was fun." She realized as soon as the words were out that it had been quite some time since she uttered those particular words. It had, indeed, been fun, and she was quite happy with her decision to come to the dance.

He took Lottie's arm. "I believe a bit of liquid refreshment would be just the thing right about now."

When they reached the refreshment table, Lottie realized that Mr. Smith and Pamela had not followed them but were in conversation with three other people. Lottie could tell by Pamela's stance that she was uncomfortable.

"Perhaps I should rescue Lady Pamela from that group," Lottie said as she accepted a cup of lemonade from Mr. Westbrooke.

He glanced over at Mr. Smith. "I think she is doing all right. Smith can make anyone relax. He owns a very successful gambling club and can talk a miser out of his coins. I won't tell you how successful he is with the ladies because that will only send you off in Lady Pamela's direction. But be at ease, he would never do anything improper with an innocent young lady." He took the empty glass from Lottie's hand and placed it on the table. "Let's take a stroll. You worry too much about your friend."

They'd gone about half the room when two gentlemen approached them. Lottie immediately stiffened at the look on their faces. Nothing threatening, but a bit too . . . hungry was the only word that fit.

Mr. Westbrooke must have sensed it because he covered her hand on his arm and gave it a slight squeeze.

"Westbrooke, are you going to introduce us to the lady?"

Mr. Westbrooke hesitated slightly and then said, "Miss Danvers, may I present Lord Sterling and Mr. Clancy. Gentleman this is Miss Danvers."

"I say, Miss Danvers, you do look familiar." Lord Sterling took her hand and kissed the air above it and studied her a bit too closely for her comfort. "Do you spend much time in London?"

"No. Not at all." She withdrew her hand from his and placed it behind her back. She knew she sounded breathless and wanted more than anything to race from the room and return home. She turned to Mr. Westbrooke. "I think I would enjoy a cup of lemonade."

He gave no indication that they had just had a glass but instead nodded to the two men. "If you will excuse us."

"Wait just a minute, Westbrooke. We're not going to let you hog this beauty all night." Lord Sterling looked in her direction. "May I request a dance, Miss Danvers."

"And I as well." Mr. Clancy smiled brightly, and she broke into a sweat. Oh, God, what was she to do now? Lord Sterling thought she looked familiar and she knew why. If she spent any time with him, he would surely make the connection.

"I'm sorry, my lord, but I am feeling quite lightheaded. I think it's the heat in here." She turned and gave Mr. Westbrooke a pleading look.

He returned a warm smile then turned toward the two men. "Some other time, Sterling. I think I will escort Miss Danvers outside for a bit of air."

"Yes. A bit of air is probably best for the young lady. We will accompany you," Mr. Clancy said.

There was nothing to be done for it. If she insisted they not join her, it would cause too much attention and that was the last thing she wanted. "Very well."

The four of them made their way to the French doors that

led to a gravel pathway. Lottie turned to see Pamela dancing with another gentleman. She didn't look at all distressed, so Lottie assumed she didn't have to worry about her friend. What she did notice was that Mr. Smith didn't look pleased at all as he watched Pamela and her partner.

Lottie only had to worry about herself and this man who thought she looked familiar.

5

CARTER WAS HAVING A HECK OF A TIME FIGURING OUT MISS Danvers. She froze when Sterling and Clancy approached them and even asked for another glass of lemonade just so she could get away. He would love to believe that was because she only wanted to spend time with him, but his inbred modesty would not allow that.

It was clear the two men made her nervous. Just as he still hadn't figured out why she'd been upset when he mentioned his brother and father, he tried to pin down when she became distressed this time. It was when he introduced Lord Sterling. Again, it was the nobility issue, he was certain.

There was something about the upper class that caused her to retreat into herself or attempt to escape. The four of them strolled out the door and the graveled pathway. Sterling kept up a constant chatter with Clancy popping in a word or two.

Carter was too aware of Miss Danvers for inane conversation.

"Miss Danvers, I must say once again that you are very

familiar. Do you have family in London that you might have visited?" Sterling continued to stare at her until Carter wanted to plant the man a facer.

"No. No one. I never go to London."

Of course, Carter knew that to be a blatant lie since they'd just returned from Berkshire's wedding. But he was not about to dispute her claim when she obviously did not want to admit to it.

"I'm finding the air quite chilly." Miss Danvers was, indeed, shivering so they all headed back to the ballroom.

"Ah, now I get to claim my dance." Before Carter could stop him, Sterling took Miss Danvers' arm and led her to the dance floor. The minstrels began a country dance, which separated the couples into two lines.

Carter stood on the sidelines, barely holding a conversation with Clancy since his attention was riveted on Miss Danvers. Every time Sterling spoke to her, she shook her head. It was apparent she was growing quite agitated.

"Excuse me," Carter said, stepping away from Clancy. He walked up to Sterling and tapped him on the shoulder. "My turn, Sterling."

The man looked surprised, then annoyed, but good manners had him stepping back. He gave a slight bow and Carter took his place. He looked over at Miss Danvers and winked. She smiled back and the dance continued.

He loved being a knight to her damsel in distress.

Carter, Lady Pamela, and Miss Danvers settled into his carriage and after he gave the signal, the driver left the front of the Assembly Rooms. Pleasant conversation continued among the three, but Carter was aware that Miss Danvers seemed out of sorts. He seemed to always be aware of her. He still wondered about her sad eyes.

Although he'd rescued her from Sterling, she had

remained on guard for the rest of their time at the dance. Eventually, when she turned down another gentleman who wanted to dance with her, she asked Carter if they could depart, stating she had the beginning of a megrim. Lady Pamela seemed ready to leave also, so they made their way to the carriage.

They came to a rolling stop in front of Lady Pamela's boarding house first and Carter escorted her to her door. She thanked him, and he was pleased to note she hardly stuttered at all. Perhaps she was becoming more comfortable with him and considered him a friend.

Once he returned to the carriage and the vehicle began to move, he took a deep breath and said, "Miss Danvers can you tell me why you were so upset with Lord Sterling?"

Her face immediately grew red. "I was not upset with Lord Sterling."

"Yes. You were." He offered her a soft smile, but his words were strong enough that she glanced out the window at the darkness rather than look at him. Taking a chance, he leaned forward, took her hands in his and tugged until she landed on the seat next to him.

"Mr. Westbrooke!" Although she attempted to look shocked, he saw a glimmer of humor in her eyes.

"Carter, if you will. Can I please persuade you to call me by my given name?" He held onto her hands to keep her from moving back across the space. She curled her fingers into a fist and her lips tightened.

He placed his knuckle under her chin and turned her face toward him. "You've given me the impression that you regard the nobility with disdain. Not just Lord Sterling, but all the lords and ladies. Particularly the lords."

She shook her head and tried to remove her hands, but he wouldn't let go.

"No. That is not true." There was almost a sense of pleading in her tone. Whatever was it that disturbed her so. Had she been abused?

Just the thought of this beautiful sweet woman being misused by a man was enough to send him searching for the cad and beating him to a pulp.

Since he saw no point in arguing about the matter as it would only upset her further, he wrapped his arm around her shoulders and pulled her body against his. "I hope that since we are friends you would share with me any difficulties you had with Lord Sterling. Did he say something to insult you?"

She edged away from him, and he loosened his grip. He did not want her to feel as though she had anything to fear from him.

It took him barely a few seconds to realize she was crying.

"Miss Danvers?"

"Yes." She looked up at him, her eyes bright with tears. "That is me." She switched from distress to anger. "At least I always thought that was me, but now I'm no longer sure." She wiped the tears from her face, and once again the sadness returned. "I'm no longer sure of anything." She slowly shook her head.

He pushed a curl behind her ear that had become loose. "What is wrong, Lottie? Can I help?" Her name just slipped out. It was how he thought of her—and he thought of her a great deal—and for some reason, it appeared that right now her last name troubled her.

Ignoring his slip in addressing her, she said, "No one can help me." She turned her face toward him, and he could not help himself. She was so beautiful in the soft light bathing her face from the lantern on the wall of the carriage. Her creamy cheeks were flushed, her eyelashes clumped with tears. He gently cupped her cheeks in his hands and lowered his head, covering her perfect lips with his.

Within seconds, he was sure he had reached heaven. She was all he had hoped she would be. Her lips were soft, warm, and moist. He nudged her mouth with his tongue expecting to be bitten, but instead she opened for him. He pulled her closer, so her soft breasts were pressed up against his coat. Carter cursed the clothing separating them, wanting to feel her warm skin next to his.

She tasted better than he'd imagined, and his imagination was quite strong. He shifted their bodies and slanted her head so he could go deeper with the kiss. Tentative at first, Lottie soon made her own exploration, tangling lightly with his tongue.

Her slight moans increased his desire, her enthusiasm delightful. Carter pulled back and looked her in the eyes. Her eyes were round—surprise or anger?—and she stared at his mouth, tempting him to taste her again.

Hoping to avoid a set-down, he said, "If what I just did upsets you, please let me know."

He held his breath as she licked her lips and slowly shook her head as if not quite sure. "No. I don't think so."

He breathed a sigh of relief. A quick glance out the window told him they still had some time before they would arrive at her building. "Please understand that I will never let anyone hurt you. I know we haven't known each other long, but you must admit there is something between us."

She began to shake her head. "No. You don't understand."

He smiled at her. "Are you denying that, Miss Danvers?"

She sighed and closed her eyes, which gave him the opportunity to kiss her again. And kiss her, he did. His mouth explored hers, touching, tasting, nipping, soothing. As much as he wanted to strip all her clothes off and plunge into her warm moistness, he was satisfied with just holding her and feeling her safe in his arms.

Never had he been satisfied with mere kisses, always anxious to take the next step. Miss Danvers was different. An innocent. A sweet gently reared young woman who he was growing more and more fond of every day.

He pulled back and ran his knuckle down her soft cheek. "I care for you, Lottie. Very much so. We have a lot in common, and you know there is a bond between us. There has been since you dumped your wine on me." He grinned when she smiled. "With your permission, I would like to court you."

Her sad eyes returned, and she offered him a forlorn smile. "No. I am afraid that is not possible."

Had she stated that emphatically, he would have stopped, but her reluctance was evident in the sorrow on her face.

"I don't know what is troubling you, or what happened in your life that is making you so very sad, but can you trust me?"

The carriage came to a slow stop in front of her building. "Lottie?"

She pulled back and shook her head. "No. I-I don't think it would work. You deserve much more than me." Before he could respond to that strange remark, she turned and fumbled with the door, jumping from the carriage before he could even assist her. She stumbled and went down on one knee, quickly recovering, and moved forward.

"Lottie!" He jumped out after her, but she scurried up the steps and quickly opened the outside door, slamming it in his face without even turning around as he reached the top step.

What the hell just happened?

LOTTIE RESTED HER CHIN ON HER PROPPED-UP HAND AND STARED

into the mirror over the dressing table in her bedroom. The Assembly the night before had been a disaster.

She feared Lord Sterling would eventually figure out why she looked familiar. The repeated questions he badgered her with during their dance almost had her walking off the floor. Thankfully, Carter seemed to notice her distress and rescued her.

Once again.

It surprised her that now she thought of him as Carter. After all, how could one continue to call a gentleman, Mr. Westbrooke, when said gentleman had kissed her senseless?

And senseless she had been. After that wonderful—and her first ever—kiss, she felt warm, happy, and contented. That was the sort of thing young girls dreamed of, and some were fortunate enough to have. A man who cared for them and gave them impressive kisses.

And then after he'd saved her from that dreadful man, she'd made a fool of herself by running off when he asked to court her. It was a simple request, and probably one he felt was innocuous enough to certainly not have her fleeing like the hounds of hell were after her.

He must think her a total ninny.

Now she was faced with church service—which she tried to never miss—and running into Carter and having to face him.

Church services in the small chapel, the students had attended in France, were much more elaborate than the services in England, but she still derived a great deal of peace when she worshiped.

She took a deep breath and picked up her brush to fix her hair. She felt as though her safe little world was crumbling. What if she had to flee Bath as she had London?

Despite Lottie's insistence that she could support herself,

Mama had continued to send her money each month. The money was sitting in a bank account in Bath, untouched. If she found it necessary to once again leave her home, she would be forced to use that money. The little bit she earned from instructing young ladies on proper behavior barely kept her fed and a roof over her head.

6

As always, she walked the distance from her flat to the church. It was a lovely day and the brisk cool air felt good on her face. She spoke briefly to the greeters at the door and found a seat near the middle. As was her habit, she picked up the hymnal sitting on the shelf below the pew in front of her.

"Good morning, Miss Danvers." So engrossed was she in the book, she jumped when Mr. Westbrooke slid in alongside her. She moved over to give him more room, or perhaps to put more space between them.

She felt the heat start in her middle and travel rapidly up her body until she was sure her face was bright enough to direct a ship to shore. "Good morning, Mr. Westbrooke." She immediately dropped the hymnal, bent to retrieve it, and banged her head on the pew in front of her.

"Allow me." Mr. Westbrooke touched her arm to keep her from moving. Oh, how she wished she could crawl away and return home, never to show her face again. Why he continued to show interest in her with all her bumbling and running away and generally acting like a fool baffled her.

He picked up the book and handed it to her just as the

vicar began the service. She took a deep breath and flipped through the pages until she found the correct hymn at the same time the congregation ceased singing.

She made herself sit absolutely still during the sermon, tithing, and Communion. If she didn't move a muscle perhaps, she would not make a laughingstock of herself any more than she already had.

"May I entice you to join me for a light luncheon, Miss Danvers?" They had just nodded to the vicar and stepped out into the sunshine. Lottie was so torn. She really liked Mr. Westbrooke, but there was nowhere this friendship could go. Encouraging him was not fair.

"I don't think that is a good idea." Her half-hearted response did not seem to discourage him.

He leaned in, close to her ear. "What if I promise not to kiss you again?" He stepped back and regarded her with raised eyebrows.

Blast! There went the heat from her middle again. Except this time, it wasn't only embarrassment, but more a sense of awareness of Mr. Westbrooke; a memory of his kiss and how much she'd enjoyed it. Along with the heat was a distinct, unfamiliar tingle in her breasts and the area between her legs. Places to which she'd never given much thought.

She raised her chin. "I hardly remember that kiss at all." As soon as the words left her mouth, she wanted to bring them back. Especially when he grinned, knowing full well the kiss was emblazoned on her mind.

Although she was a novice at such things no doubt Mr. Westbrooke had kissed many women and knew when the lady had been affected by his kiss.

And she definitely had been.

"Oh, very well. I will accept your invitation." She cringed at how impolite that sounded. She continued to do things around this man that would appall her students. When she wasn't tripping over everything. The man definitely had the ability to rattle her.

He bowed. "Thank you." He extended his arm. "My carriage is around the corner.

They strolled along, with Mr. Westbrooke making small talk. Lottie was usually very good at it, but not now, as she was still uncomfortable about their last parting. But Mr. West-brooke acted as if nothing was wrong with the fact that she only nodded at all his comments.

He seemed to also forget, or pretend to forget, her unlady-like departure when he brought her home after the dance the night before. She was torn between frustration that he wouldn't give up on her and admiration for his tenaciousness.

"Where is your friend, Lady Pamela?"

"She generally attends church with me, but once in a while she ignores her alarm clock and misses the service." She grinned. "I would say this is one of those days."

He'd directed his driver to bring them to a small restaurant on Milsom Place, one of Lottie's favorite areas in Bath to take an afternoon stroll with all the shops and eateries there.

"I hope this meets with your approval?" He held his hand out as she stepped from the carriage.

"Yes. I love this restaurant but have only eaten here once or twice." She didn't add it was too expensive for her purse and had to save several weeks to be able to join her two friends there.

He opened the door to the restaurant to allow her to enter. "It is one of my favorites as well."

He apparently had eaten there several times since he was well-known among the staff. They were led to a lovely table near the front windows which allowed a good amount of light since the day had turned cloudy.

The room only held about a dozen tables, and most of them were full. Wonderful scents came from the kitchen each time a server entered or left the dining room to fetch food.

"What looks good to you?" Mr. Westbrook asked as Lottie perused the menu.

"Everything," she said and grinned. "I am quite hungry."

"Then I am particularly happy that I invited you to join me for luncheon." He returned his attention to the menu, both of them remaining silent as they read over the choices.

"Have you decided yet?" The waiter stood at their table, his pad and pencil at the ready.

"Miss Danvers?" Mr. Westbrooke asked.

She hadn't been exaggerating when she said everything looked good and that she was quite hungry. However, making a glutton of herself was not well done. "I believe I will have the roasted beef."

"Ah. A very good choice," the waiter said as he noted her selection. "And for you sir?"

"I believe the lady has made a good selection, and I will have the same." Mr. Westbrooke closed his menu and handed it over to the waiter who made a slight bow and left them.

CARTER STUDIED LOTTIE AS THE WAITER TOOK HIS LEAVE AND returned to the kitchen to fetch their food. Given the abrupt way they'd parted the night before, he'd been pleasantly surprised to find her in church. And even more pleased to find she didn't hit him over the head with the hymnal.

Although he found her behavior confusing, he continued to believe she had something in her past—something to do with nobility—that kept her on edge. Sometimes she was completely relaxed and other times he could almost see the tension start and the fear in her eyes.

He found it quite difficult to understand why she abruptly raced from a gentleman requesting to court her. Did she truly expect to spend her life away from society, teaching young ladies' deportment? That was no life for a beautiful young woman and would certainly not pay very well.

What had happened in her life to put her on that path?

However, given how distraught she'd become when he asked to court her, he considered it quite a boon that she had agreed to join him for luncheon. If he were to move forward with what he hoped to be courtship, followed by marriage, he had to tread lightly. For whatever reason, she was quite skittish.

Most ladies liked to talk about themselves, so perhaps some conversation along the lines of her work might get her to open up a bit more. There was no doubt in his mind that she was hiding something that troubled her a great deal. His mind kept returning to a broken heart, or perhaps an occurrence even more sinister, which always managed to raise his ire when he considered it.

"How many students do you teach?" That seemed to be quite an innocuous question.

She must have thought so too because she offered him a soft smile. "I currently have six young ladies. Four of them will make their debut in London when the next Season starts. The other two have another year, but their mothers wanted them to have extra time to be prepared."

"And what comprises your lessons?" He nodded at the waiter who placed their food in front of them. Delicious roasted beef, along with Yorkshire pudding, gravy, mushy peas, and boiled potatoes and carrots. He also placed a small, warm loaf of bread with a crock of butter on the table.

As they began to eat, Lottie talked about her students, each of their strengths and weaknesses and what they needed to accomplish to be successful on the Marriage Mart. Her eyes lit up as she talked, obviously loving the world that the girls were intended for.

But from what she said, not a world she intended for herself. *Why?* But his caution led him to silence and instead enjoyed her conversation.

Suddenly, Carter had a wonderful idea that would move his courtship along without Lottie suspecting his intents. "I say, it would seem to me that having a gentleman on hand to help the girls learn how to converse in Society might make a difference in their training. I find so many of the young ladies making their come-outs seem to be a bit—shall we say—shy? I've met some who could hardly speak of more than hair ribbons and gown colors."

Lottie sat very still and studied him. Had he pushed too far, too fast? When a slow smile spread across her face, he relaxed. She wasn't jumping up and racing from the room.

"That is a wonderful idea." She raised her eyebrows. "I don't suppose you would be volunteering to help, would you?" Her smirk told him she knew exactly what he was doing but didn't seem upset by his suggestion.

He grinned back and gave a slight bow. "I am at your service, Miss Danvers."

"It must be someplace public so as not to cause any sort of a scandal."

"How about tea in the Pump Room?"

"Perfect! I can watch them closely to see how they conduct themselves in public, how they take their tea, engage in conversation, and make a good impression." Lottie tapped her lips with her fingertip. "I believe taking two girls out at a time would work best. If we had all six of them together it would be too difficult to assess each girl's behavior."

Carter placed his napkin alongside his plate and sat back.

Thank goodness she suggested only two girls at a time. He nearly panicked at the thought of six young ladies all giggling and fluttering their eyelashes at him.

"Then it is settled. Just let me know when and I will arrive at your home to escort you and two young ladies to tea."

"But you have a business to run, Mr. Westbrooke."

"Indeed, I do. But I can make time in my day to help young ladies be successful in their hunt for a husband."

Lottie's lips tightened. "I hate that term. It makes it all seem so cold, so calculating. I picture young girls with a bow and arrow pointed at some gentleman who is trying his best to escape.

"I prefer to think that the girls will be enjoying a social life while they decide if the gentleman paying them court is the one they care to spend the rest of their lives with."

"Ah, I believe you are a romantic, Miss Danvers."

She hesitated long enough that he began to think she would not answer him. Then she said, "Not exactly a romantic, Mr. Westbrooke, but I simply want more for my girls than what some of their parents do."

He reached across the table and covered her hand with his. "I like to think we are friends."

She looked surprised at the turn of conversation. "I-I guess so."

"Then please let us dispense with the formality. I would like for you to call me Carter, and I hope to gain your permission to call you Lottie." He grinned. "I love that name, you know. It suits you so very well."

"It's really Charlotte, you know. Once I began my new life in Bath, I changed it to Lottie. Actually, it was my two friends' idea. However, with regard to your request, though I still think it is improper, perhaps when no one is around to hear us, it might be acceptable. But I don't understand why it is important to you."

Despite knowing precisely why it was important to him, he remained silent. If he again mentioned his intention to court her and eventually—hopefully— marry her, he would most likely end up chasing her down the streets of Bath.

"Let's just say I feel that it's something that friends would do. For example, do you call Lady Pamela by that title? Or now that Miss Mallory is Lady Berkshire, will you be calling her that?"

"No." She laughed. "All right, Mr. Westbro—rather, Carter. You have made your point."

"May I interest you in dessert?" The waiter had returned and began to remove their dishes.

"I would certainly like some of that blancmange on the menu." Carter looked over at Lottie. "What will you have?"

"I probably shouldn't have dessert after that wonderful meal, but I cannot pass up the Victoria sponge."

"Tea, also, if you will," Carter added.

"When shall we take our first couple of young ladies to the Pump Room?" Carter was anxious to pin Lottie down before she came up with another excuse not to see him again.

"I will look at my schedule and consult with the girls. Is it all right if I send a note around? If the day and time doesn't fit into your schedule, please do not put off your work to help me. We can always do it another time."

He continued to stare at her mesmerizing mouth as she spoke. He wanted very badly to lean across the table and cover her lips with his. No other woman had ever affected him this way. He wanted her so badly he couldn't eat, sleep, or work without thoughts of her invading his mind.

"My schedule is flexible. I am sure whatever time you select I will be available. After all, we are preparing young ladies for successful matches. That is truly a worthy cause. Is it not?"

He didn't care for the slight flush that covered Lottie's face, but just then the waiter arrived with their tea and dessert, ending the conversation. She smiled up at the waiter and thanked him.

Carter was jealous of the waiter.

He'd fallen hard.

7

CARTER WAVED AT GRAYSON, LORD BERKSHIRE, AS HE ENTERED Boodle's, an exclusive gentlemen's club on Pall Mall in London. They had arranged to meet to discuss a new business venture they were considering.

"Well, aren't you looking very much the happy groom!" Carter took the seat across from Grayson in the dining area of the club. The room was full of other diners, men who had business to attend to, and a few of the idle nobility who had not yet come to realize that the world was changing and unless they changed with it, they would find themselves in dire straits.

At least a few of them understood the situation and had married young ladies from America with large dowries.

"Yes. Much to my surprise, I find marriage agrees with me. Once we are passed the blasted court hearing—which is tomorrow—my wife and I will be able to return to Bath where we both prefer to be."

"I find I must agree with you. I was never fond of London, and only come during the Season to make a necessary appearance in Parliament."

The waiter approached their table, pen and pad in hand. "What will please you this morning, gentlemen?"

"I will have a full breakfast. With plenty of tea." Carter nodded at Grayson. "Same for you, I assume?"

"Yes. I am quite hungry this morning. Except make mine coffee instead of tea."

Once the waiter was on his way with their order, Grayson said, "Anything of interest pop up while I was on my wedding trip?"

"No. I have the papers with me that my man of business drew up for our consideration on this new shipping contract." Carter leaned over and picked up his satchel and withdrew several papers. "It's all there." He handed the papers to Grayson.

Grayson looked over the documents, asking a question or two as the waiter placed two plates of beans, eggs, sausage, bacon, fried tomatoes, fried mushrooms, and toast in front of them. The aroma from the food smelled wonderful and Carter was anxious to partake.

The papers were put aside as the men dug into their food, the conversation consisting of compliments on their meal. Once they were finished, and the empty plates removed, Carter pulled his teacup closer, rested his forearms on the table, and looked over at Grayson. "Tell me what you know about Miss Danvers."

Carter noted that Grayson did not seem surprised. "Addie's friend?"

"Yes."

Grayson leaned back in his chair. "So, my wife was correct. There is interest there on your part."

Carter sighed. "Yes. I am not afraid to state there is a great deal of interest. The woman fascinates me, and after all these years of dodging the marriage-minded mamas, I think wedding bells are on the horizon for me. At least I hope so."

"My goodness," Grayson said, a grin growing on his face. "It sounds as though you have it bad, my friend."

Carter shrugged. "Indeed. It is a bit funny when you recall how adamant I've been about love at first sight and romance in general. However, I am not having an easy time of it with the young lady."

Grayson swallowed a sip of coffee. "What seems to be the problem? Is the lady not interested?"

Carter shook his head. "That's the issue. I'm quite certain there is interest there, but she is skittish, almost as if there is something in her background that frightened her."

Grayson nodded his thanks at the waiter who poured more coffee into his cup. "I wish I could tell you more about Miss Danvers, but the only thing Addie has shared with me is that Miss Danvers had some sort of a break with her mother, who lives in London, and moved to Bath shortly thereafter.

"My wife also tells me that Miss Danvers is quite reluctant to attend any sort of public event, which Addie thinks has to do with her not wanting to be recognized."

Carter leaned back; his brows drawn together. "How odd. Recognized, eh? She is a beautiful woman, and the time I've spent with her proves her to also be kind, witty, and quite intelligent. She was well educated in a private school in France."

Grayson spread his fingers on the table and shrugged. "I wish I could give you more information, but that is all I know. To be honest, I don't know for sure if Addie knows any more than that, either. Miss Danvers is a bit of an enigma."

Carter finished his tea and placed his napkin on the table. "I am off this morning to catch the mid-morning rail back to Bath." He pushed his chair back and stood.

"I wish I could have given you more information, but I'm afraid there isn't much more to give. I agree that she is quite lovely, and her personality does seem charming. All I can say is that I wish you the best of luck with your pursuit of Miss Danvers."

"Thank you. I really dislike going behind the woman's back to gather information, but she is reluctant to discuss her personal life."

They walked to the door and took their coats and hats from the doorman. Once they stepped out into the London foggy air, Carter said, "I wish you well with the hearing." He finished buttoning his coat against the cold December air.

"As I wish you well with your courtship of Miss Danvers," Grayson added.

On those words, they parted, and Carter hailed a hackney to take him to Paddington Station. Normally he would walk the less than three miles, but he didn't want to miss the rail.

He considered his courtship of Miss Danvers. If it could be termed that. It was definitely a two steps forward, one step back situation. He knew without a doubt that she was attracted to him. Life experience had taught him that. But why she was holding back, and at times seemed almost frightened, baffled him, while at the same time raised his indignation on her behalf.

No matter how many times he considered her behavior, he always came back to members of the nobility. Something must have happened to her and another 'gentleman' that sent her running to Bath and hiding from the public. Perhaps the next time he was in London, he would drop her name and see if he could gather any information that way.

He was looking forward to the next day when he was to meet with Lottie and two of her students, Miss Waverly and Miss Dobson, both daughters of barons. They would be making their come-out in a couple of months when the Season began in London. Playing host to two giggling young ladies was not his idea of an interesting way to spend his afternoon, but if it gave him more time with Lottie, then he was happy to do it.

He spent the rail ride home to Bath thinking of various ways he could maneuver Lottie into attending a few social occasions. He didn't mind biding his time if that's what she needed to feel comfortable with him.

If only he knew what plagued the poor girl.

LOTTIE INSPECTED MISS DOBSON AND MISS WAVERLY AS THEY waited for Carter to arrive. He would escort them to the tea shop on Milsom Street. "Now remember all the etiquette I taught you, and please make polite conversation with Mr. Westbrooke."

"Is he your beau, Miss Danvers?" Miss Waverly asked.

"Heavens, no." Lottie felt a blush rise from her middle all the way to her hairline. "He is just a friend."

"Mama said men and women could not be friends." Miss Dobson added.

"I don't wish to disparage your mother, Miss Dobson, but men and women can be friends. Mr. Westbrooke and I prove that." She hated that she sounded so supercilious, but she did not want to think of Carter in any other role, and truth be known, she wasn't entirely comfortable in the role of friends.

Before they could continue the discussion on male and female friends, there was a slight knock on her door. "That must be Mr. Westbrooke now. Remember your manners, girls. I will be watching you, and when it's over I will let you know how you did."

Lottie opened the door and as always, took in a deep

breath at the sight of Mr. Carter Westbrooke. Handsome as ever, he wore a light charcoal pair of trousers, with a deep blue vest, white shirt, and black ascot. Over his jacket, he wore a warm dark coat of superfine wool.

Miss Dobson and Miss Waverly both giggled. Lottie shot them a stern look and they immediately stiffened and assumed the stance ladies of the *ton* were expected to affect in public. Aloof and a bit of ennui. But not too much for young ladies. They were still supposed to be excited about being at all the events they'd been banned from before they debuted.

"Ladies, you look wonderful." Carter bowed and took Lottie's hand first, then looked expectantly at the two girls.

"Ladies, may I make known to you, Mr. Westbrooke." He bowed and Lottie continued. "Mr. Westbrooke, may I present Miss Dobson and Miss Waverly." Both girls did a respectful curtsy which made Lottie very happy. She noticed they both blushed furiously when Carter took their hands and kissed the backs.

"Ladies, my carriage awaits you. Shall we proceed?" Carter took Lottie's arm and proceeded down the stairs with the two girls following behind them to his carriage.

He helped each woman in, then climbed in and tapped the ceiling of the carriage to signal the driver. Lottie nodded to Miss Waverly.

"Mr. Westbrooke, have you lived in Bath long?" The young girl managed to ask the question without blushing or giggling. Well done.

"Yes, Miss Waverly. I have been a resident of our fair town for quite some time. I assume this has been your home all your life?"

"Yes. My parents preferred to keep my sisters and myself away from the London air."

Lottie mouthed 'well done' to Miss Waverly and then turned toward Miss Dobson.

"Um, Mr. Westbrooke." Deep breath. "Do you have a dog?" Miss Dobson blushed furiously and gulped as Lottie looked in her direction, her brows raised.

Carter, thankfully, did not laugh at the poor girl, but merely said, "No. I do not have a dog. Do you, Miss Dobson?"

She let out a deep breath. "Yes. I do. His name is Walter and he is a Pekingese. His name is Walter. Oh, yes I already said that." Her voice faded away as she grew a deeper shade of red.

Carter kept his expression pleasant, but Lottie could almost see his shoulders shaking, trying to hold in the laugh that she had a hard time controlling herself.

"Mr. Westbrooke is a fan of history, which I know you enjoy quite a bit, Miss Waverly."

Both Lottie and Carter turned toward the girl who just looked back. Finally, she said, "I know all the kings and queens. Would you care to have me recite them?"

Thankfully the coach came to a stop and Lottie let out a sigh of relief. "Here we are girls."

Carter jumped out and turned to assist Lottie first, then the two girls. They proceeded into the tearoom. Once they were seated, each girl watched Lottie as she took her napkin and placed it on her lap. They copied her movements while Carter looked on with amusement.

They placed an order for tea, sandwiches, and biscuits and Lottie carried the conversation, including the two girls. She was startled by the arrival of a gentleman at their table. It didn't take her long to recognize Lord Sterling, the man she'd met at the Assembly who thought she looked so familiar.

Her breathing immediately sped up and she knew her face flushed. It appeared Carter noticed it, as well.

"Good afternoon, Westbrooke, ladies." Sterling glanced at them all, but his attention swung directly to Lottie. "It's is nice to see you again, Miss Danvers."

"Thank you." Her voice was clipped, and she knew the girls were confused as to why she didn't return his statement with a similar one of her own. Her leg began to jump as she waited for him to say something in front of everyone.

"What brings you here, Sterling?" Carter had been watching her closely and attempted to bring Sterling's attention back to him. Thankfully, her two charges were busy with pouring their tea and passing the plate of offerings. If they noticed anything odd about their teacher, they didn't show it.

"I like to stop for a bit of tea in the afternoon. I would ask to join you, but I've just finished and am on my way now to my club."

Lottie kept her eyes downcast, studying her cup of tea as if she'd never seen one before.

"I say, Miss Danvers, I continue to believe I know you from somewhere." Lord Sterling studied her in a way that made her extremely uncomfortable.

A quick glance at Lottie and Carter jumped in. "If you will excuse us, Sterling, the ladies and I are about to enjoy our tea. Nice of you to stop by."

"Yes. Just so. I will see you around." Lord Sterling made a slight bow and with one final look at Lottie turned and left the tearoom.

Any appetite Lottie had for the tea and biscuits walked out the door with Lord Sterling.

Although Carter didn't question her, he continued to watch her throughout their time there. He kept up a steady chatter with the girls, for which Lottie was thankful, since she seemed to have lost her ability to conduct a conversation.

The girls, however, did not seem to notice for which she

was grateful. Whatever was she going to do about that man? It would be only a matter of time before he realized who she was. She would have to leave Bath. That thought almost reduced her to tears.

Not only did she not want to give up her lovely flat and her friends but starting over again would be difficult. Is that something she would have to do for the rest of her life? If she had to leave Bath, it would be best to move to Wales or Scotland. It was highly unlikely anyone in those places would know her mother.

Once again, the anger at her mother and what she did to ruin Lottie's life rose to the surface. Would she never get over that? She startled when Carter called her name. "Are you well, Miss Danvers?"

Both girls stared at her and she looked down at her plate, it was still full of the small sandwiches and biscuits. "Yes. I am fine, Mr. Westbrooke. I am afraid I was woolgathering. Please excuse my poor manners."

It appeared while she was wallowing in self-pity, the other three had finished their tea and were ready to leave.

"I guess it is time for us to depart," she said. She patted her mouth and placed her napkin alongside her plate. Lottie gracefully rose and the two girls and Mr. Westbrooke followed.

They made their way to the carriage with Carter taking her arm and tucking it alongside his body. He leaned in close to her and spoke softly. "Miss Danvers, sometime soon I would like to have a conversation with you. I know something is bothering you and even frightening you. I want to help."

Dear God. No.

8

CARTER DROPPED THE KNOCKER ON THE FRONT DOOR OF THE building where Lottie had her flat. Since the rooms were only let to women, there was a man who monitored the outside door, which made Carter extremely happy to know that Lottie was safe.

"Good afternoon, sir. May I ask who you are visiting?" The older man wore a simple footman's uniform. He stepped back to allow Carter to enter.

Carter removed his hat and nodded to the man. "I would like to visit with Miss Danvers."

"Very good, sir. However, I must ask you to wait in the parlor and I will fetch Miss Danvers. We do not allow gentlemen above the ground floor." The man waved toward a room to the right side of the entrance hall.

Carter did not avail himself of a seat, but as he wandered the room, he took note of the well-decorated space that was obviously meant to provide a place for a woman to meet with a guest. He was feeling even better about Lottie's building.

Within five minutes, Lottie entered the room. "Good afternoon, Mr. Westbrooke. To what do I owe this *surprise*—she emphasized the word—visit?"

Her words might have been terse, but the look on her face was anything but annoyed. In fact, he could say that she almost seemed happy to see him.

"I'm sorry I didn't send a note around, but I happen to find myself near your flat and thought you might want to join me for tea. Or a ride in the park. Or a stroll around the neighborhood." Hopefully, he didn't sound as desperate as he felt, waiting for her to frown and refuse.

She hesitated for a few moments and then, to his utter surprise, said, "Yes. I think I would enjoy a stroll. So far, I've been cooped up here for the entire day with one student after another. It will be good to have a bit of fresh air."

Since it would be the epitome of inelegance to hop into the air and shout with glee, Carter merely smiled and bowed. "Thank you."

"Just let me get my cape." And with those few words, Lottie was back out the door, leaving him with a warm feeling, mixed with excitement at how well his request had gone.

Luckily, it was a rare sunny day and even though they were nearing the end of winter, the air wasn't too unpleasant. They strolled the area around her neighborhood, making light conversation.

"Were you pleased with your students' performance at tea the other day?" Carter stopped their stroll as they approached the end of the pavement. With no vehicles headed their way, they crossed the street and continued.

"Yes. For the most part, I thought they did quite well. Poor Miss Dobson was near tears when she arrived the next day for her lesson. Her question about whether you owned a dog was certainly not the sort of thing I teach as a method to employ while making polite conversation. I had to assure her more than once that it was not a major *faux pas* since you were, for the most part, a test subject."

"Both young ladies seemed to be very sweet. I am sure they will do well with you leading them." He looked in her direction, waiting for her reaction to his next question. "Will you be acting as their chaperone, then, when they make their debut in London?"

Lottie sucked in a deep breath and shook her head furiously. "No. Not at all. My time with them ends right before they leave for London."

He placed his hand on hers, hoping to keep her from bolting since her reaction to his question was what he'd expected. "How odd. I would think their parents would continue your employment when they entered the Marriage Mart."

"No. I made it quite clear when they engaged me that I would not act as a chaperone." She glanced at him sideways. "After all, I have other students who need my services here in Bath."

Good response, my dear Miss Danvers. One point for you.

"And, of course, you dislike London." He looked at a store window, attempting to appear as though this was merely conversation and he was not looking for information.

Again, the stiffening of her body. "Yes. I dislike London."

He took a deep breath, deciding *in for a penny, in for a pound.* "And you don't wish to be recognized in London, either."

Lottie came to an abrupt stop. He attempted to look innocent, but he doubted he'd succeeded.

"What do you mean?" Her breathing had increased, and her face was growing redder by the moment. "Why would you say that?"

"Hmm. Maybe because you haven't worn your spectacles

since our return to Bath." He grinned at her, hoping to restore some calm. "I assume you don't need spectacles to see."

Lottie attempted to pull her arm free, but he held on tight. "Don't be upset, please."

"I am not upset. However, I need to return home. I have a student due soon." She continued to tug on her arm, and he continued to hold on.

"Let me help you, Lottie. Please."

Lottie shook her head. "I don't know what you are talking about. Everything is fine. I am fine."

Time to retreat once again. If he kept this up, he would push her further and further away, which was certainly not his intent. "Then I apologize for upsetting you. That was not my intention."

"Nonsense. As I stated, I am not upset." Her flushed face and trembling hand on his arm belied her statement.

"Let us return to you home, then, so you may meet your next student." He turned them so they headed back the way they had come. He had to find a way to calm her before he let her go or he would most likely find a slammed door in his face the next time he attempted to call on her.

Her pace was considerably faster than before his challenge, but by the time they arrived at her building, she was a bit calmer. He even got her to smile at one of his very lame jokes.

"May I call on you soon? Perhaps you would enjoy a visit to the Holbourne Museum."

The regret on her face twisted his insides. It was obvious she did not want to say no, but for some reason was about to do just that. "I am afraid I simply don't have the time for visits and strolls, Mr. Westbrooke."

He reached out and touched her chin, raising her head so he could look in her eyes. "It would do you well to understand that I do not give up easily, Lottie. I am very interested in you, and I want to court you. I can also assure you I am a gentleman and would never do anything to harm you. In any way."

When she began to shake her head, he continued. "I know you said no before, but as I said, I am quite tenacious. Unless you tell me unconditionally that you have no interest in me at all, I will try very hard to persuade you to allow us time together to get to know each other."

To his shock, tears filled her eyes. "You do not want to get to know me, Mr. Westbrooke. Of that I am certain."

Before he could stop her, she raced up the stairs, and after a quick knock, the door was opened and quickly closed behind her.

TWO DAYS LATER, LOTTIE AND ONE OF HER NEWER STUDENTS, Lady Edwina, the daughter of Viscount Monroe, climbed into the viscount's carriage for a ride to Milsom Street. There they would take tea at the tearoom in Jolly's Department Store, one of the finer stores in Bath.

They chatted for a while, then fell quiet, just the rhythmic sound of the horses' hooves on the cobblestones reaching them, leaving Lottie with her own thoughts. Thoughts that always returned to Carter. She liked him. Truth be known, quite a bit. It was obvious he cared for her, too. But every time her useless daydream of them being together snuck into her thoughts, she pushed it firmly away.

Even more troublesome were the nighttime dreams that she had no control over. She was disturbed at some of the things she had dreamed about doing with Carter. Things that involved naked bodies and a great deal of touching. Maybe she *was* her mother's daughter.

The day was not as pleasant as it had been when she and Carter had taken their stroll. The sun was hiding behind the clouds and there was a bit of a breeze. A reminder that even though the year was entering spring, it was still chilly at times.

Thinking back on their time together the other day, she was chagrined at him noticing she only wore those fake spectacles in London. It was probably a stupid thing to do anyway. Having her mother's looks and coloring, it would take more than a pair of eyeglasses to disguise her from someone who knew her mother well.

She didn't realize how much she had been woolgathering until Lady Edwina said, "Miss Danvers? I believe we are here."

Lottie moved the window curtain aside and glanced outside. "Oh, dear. Yes, we are. I apologize for my inattention."

Just then the door opened, and the driver helped her down first, then Lady Edwina. They made their way into the tea shop and were directed to a table against the wall.

There were quite a few patrons in the shop, but since this was Lady Edwina's first foray to a tea shop as a student, Lottie gave her complete attention to the girl.

They ordered tea with cucumber sandwiches and biscuits. Lottie explained the correct way to pour tea, and how to keep up polite conversation while she did so. Although Lady Edwina was only a year away from her debut, she hadn't had much in the way of Polite Society instruction since her mother was deceased and her governess hadn't encouraged her to learn the more refined arts that young ladies needed to know.

"Miss Danvers, how lovely to see you." Lord Sterling stood next to their table, a look in his eyes that frightened her. Before she could react to seeing him, he leaned in next to her ear. "Or should I call you Miss Danforth?" He stood back and grinned not knowing, or perhaps not caring, that he'd just crushed her entire world.

Lady Edwina looked toward her as if she expected Lottie to introduce her to his lordship. All Lottie could think of was getting out of the tea shop without bringing any notice to herself.

She called on all her years of training to stiffen her back and glared at the man. "I am sorry, my lord, but I am instructing this young lady in the finer art of Polite Society and I must ask you to leave us alone."

Sterling threw his head back and laughed, loud enough to attract the attention of just about everyone in the room. "*You* are instructing a young lady on Polite Society? How very amusing. Does your courtesan mother know this?"

"Miss Danvers?" Lady Edwina looked back and forth between her and Lord Sterling with confusion.

"It is nothing with which to concern yourself, my lady. However, I feel we must cut short our lesson for today." Before the poor girl could react, Lottie stood and headed toward the door. She stopped the man who had seated them earlier, not sure where their waiter was. "I'm afraid my charge and I must take our leave." She withdrew a few coins from her reticule with a shaky hand and gave them to the startled man.

Lady Edwina had caught up to her by that time and they both made their way out of the tea shop.

"Wait!" Lord Sterling was on their heels, and Lottie wished him to perdition.

He had the nerve to grasp her arm to stop her. "I want to speak to you about something that might be to your benefit."

Lottie closed her eyes, then turned to Lady Edwina. "My lady, please proceed to the carriage and I will meet you in a minute."

Still looking bewildered, the girl nodded and headed toward the carriage parked a few steps away from the store's entrance. Once Lottie was sure Lady Edwina had entered the carriage and the door closed, she turned to Lord Sterling.

"My lord, I have no idea why you continue to annoy me. Please know that I do not wish to speak with you, nor have you approach me in public."

He leaned back on his heels, his hands in his pockets. "Come now, Miss Danvers. Or whatever your name is. I knew from the first time I saw you that you looked familiar. You are Mrs. Danforth's daughter. And please do not deny it since you look exactly like her."

There was truly no way to go but forward. She raised her chin and attempted to look bored. "And if I am?"

"Then I would like to offer you my protection. I can set you up with a house, a carriage, and all the fine clothes and jewelry you wish. Right here in Bath."

The anger coursing through her almost had her striking the man. However, with the few people who were on the public street, and especially those who watched with interest, she merely lowered her voice. "I am not for sale."

Before he could respond, she practically ran to the carriage, climbed in and tapped the ceiling for the driver to proceed.

"Are you well, Miss Danvers?" Lady Edwina studied her carefully.

"Yes, my lady. I apologize for cutting our lesson short, but I can assure you we will do it another time. Please forgive me." She took out her handkerchief and patted her upper lip.

That was about all the words she could get passed the large lump in her throat. She managed to hold onto her composure until they arrived at the Monroe townhouse, where Lottie wished Lady Edwina a good day and immediately left her to walk—and practically run—to Berkshire's house.

Addie had been busy with the bookstore since her return to London and a few weeks had actually passed since Lottie had last seen her. For now, she needed someone she could trust to pour her heart out to.

Once Lottie had been instructed by the butler to proceed upstairs to Addie's sitting room alongside her bedchamber, she hurried up the steps and entered the room, knowing her face was blotchy from crying. She twisted her handkerchief in her hands.

Addie stood and reached out her hand. "What's wrong, Lottie?"

Lottie took in a shuddering breath, having just come to the decision as she climbed the stairs to the bedchamber floor. "I have to leave Bath."

"Leave Bath! Why?" She patted the space alongside her on the lovely flowered settee.

Lottie sat and dabbed at her eyes with her handkerchief. "Because I just came from Milsom Street where I was taking tea with one of my students." Another deep breath. "Lord Sterling walked into the shop and greeted me."

Addie waited patiently for Lottie to pull herself together. "Yes?"

"Don't you see? I can't stay in Bath. Lord Sterling has moved here permanently." He hadn't said as much, but since she'd seen him so often and he offered her a house in Bath, he must be a permanent resident.

Addie took her hand. "And?"

"He knows my mother. Everyone in London knows my mother. Now everyone in Bath will as well. I must leave."

She hopped up to escape and Addie grabbed her skirt. "Wait. I don't understand."

Lottie attempted to pull away, but Addie held firm. "You came to tell me you have to leave Bath. I will not let you go until you explain why. And not just because Lord Sterling, who as far as I know has very little consequence, knows your mother."

Lottie tried to say the words, but it took her a minute to actually say them out loud to her best friend who had no idea. "My mother is Mrs. Danforth."

Stunned silence followed the words echoing around the room. Addie sucked in a deep breath. "Oh, no."

"Yes. I'm sure you've heard the name. Everyone who is anyone in London among the *ton* knows her name. Even among young girls making their debuts, who should never know about such things, Mrs. Danforth's name is whispered in ladies' retiring room."

Lottie stood and paced in front of Addie. "The most well-known courtesan in London is my mama."

"But why must you leave Bath? You have friends here and a business."

Lottie snickered. "Do you honestly believe the parents of the girls I've been instructing on how to conduct oneself in Polite Society will continue to allow me anywhere near their daughters? My living is gone. I must move again to where no one knows me, nor will ever know me."

With those words and the stunned expression on Addie's face, she fled the house with the full intention of packing her belongings and taking the first rail out of Bath.

To where she had no idea.

9

THE NEXT MORNING LOTTIE WAS INTERRUPTED IN HER PACKING by a knock on her door. Mr. Everson, the man who guarded the front door to her building, stood there, looking a tad uncomfortable. "Miss Danvers there is a gentleman and lady awaiting you downstairs. They insist they must speak with you immediately."

Exhausted from no sleep the night before, she was a bit confused. She frowned and placed her brush, comb, and small mirror in her satchel. "Did they give their names?"

"Lord Monroe and his daughter's governess, Mrs. Temple."

His lordship and the governess! Lottie's stomach cramped and her heart sped up. It was truly amazing how fast bad news could appear on one's doorstep. "Tell them I will be there momentarily."

She pulled the mirror back out of her satchel and examined herself. She looked pale and scared; the few freckles scattered across her nose standing out. There was no way out of this. She took a deep breath and left her flat.

"Good morning, my lord. Mrs. Temple." She had met the governess when his lordship had engaged her to groom his daughter for her presentation to Society. Now the woman sat on the dark brown sofa, glaring at her.

They both rose.

"I'm afraid it is not a good morning, Miss Danvers." Lord Monroe looked uneasy as he addressed her.

"I will come right to the point," Mrs. Temple said. "I have been lovely Lady Edwina's governess for years. I have protected her from the more sordid things in life. She is a sweet, innocent, young girl. However, it appears you had no hesitancy in speaking with one of your paramours while having tea with my charge."

Lottie sucked in a breath. Although she certainly had something to hide, she could not let that remark pass. "I am sorry Mrs. Temple, but first of all the gentleman—she almost choked on the word—who spoke with me yesterday was not, has never been, and will never be, my paramour. I have done nothing to be ashamed of, nor would I ever expose a young girl to the part of life to which you refer."

"Do you deny that your mother is a well-known courtesan in London?" Lord Monroe asked.

Well, then. Let's get right to the point, shall we?

"No, I don't deny that since it is true. However, I see no reason to continue this conversation." She turned to leave, but Lord Monroe said, "You are dismissed. I no longer require your services."

Since Lottie was planning on leaving today anyway, she was about to notify all her student's parents. She had hoped—apparently unsuccessfully—that they would not find out the real reason for her abrupt departure.

"I understand." There wasn't much more to be said about that.

"Have you no honor, Miss Danvers?" Mrs. Temple pointed her finger at Lottie. "I cannot imagine why you would take young girls as your charges when you come from such a sullied background."

Close to tears, Lottie said, "I am sorry you feel that way, Mrs. Temple, but I do not have a sullied background. I was raised in a private girls' school in France. I have done nothing to warrant your disdain."

"Your mother is a whore!"

Lottie's shame turned into anger at the ugly word. "How dare you! My mother took care of me all her life. She paid for an exclusive girls' school and even made the trip from London to France to see me twice a month. You know nothing about my mother."

"I know all I need to know. She paid for that school with ill-earned money." Mrs. Temple waved her finger. "You are a disgrace. You should not be allowed near young girls."

Lottie waved at the doorway. "Please leave. You have said what you need to say." Before they had a chance to go, Lottie stalked from the room and raced upstairs.

She entered her flat and leaned against the door. She took in huge gulps of air, attempting to keep the tears at bay, but lost that battle and slid down the door to sit on the floor. She pulled her legs up to her chest, leaned her forehead on her knees and sobbed.

Two hours later, she looked around her flat, making certain she had removed all of her most important things. It was impossible to pack everything she had accumulated in her time in Bath. Some of the lovely decorations she'd found at the vintage store would have to remain. As well as all her books.

She could only carry her clothes and grooming products. Perhaps she could post a note to Addie and ask her to have the rest of her things packed up and sent to her once she had a new home.

Rather than have another scene like the one earlier in the parlor downstairs, Lottie took the time to write notes to all her students' parents. Although considering her visit from Lord Monroe and his horrid governess, in time most would learn why she left in a hurry. However, she stated in her letters that a family emergency had come up and it had been necessary for her to leave Bath.

Her rent was paid up for the rest of the month, so she left a note for Mrs. Ponsoby, her landlady, relating the same story about a family emergency. Hopefully, since she still owned the flat for a couple more weeks, it would give Addie time to get her things out of the rooms before Mrs. Ponsoby rented to another tenant.

With one last look around, she drew on her cape, hat, and gloves, and picked up her satchel. She had loved this flat and had made it into a very comfortable home. Her very first home, considering she lived at school most of her life. But deep down inside, she always knew one day she would have to leave it.

Mr. Everson was at the door, as usual. He viewed her with sympathy, which told her he had heard everything that had transpired between her and her visitors.

"I must leave for a family emergency." She raised her chin, looking him in the eye. Although she was sure he knew why she was leaving, she kept up with the story she had written in Mrs. Ponsoby's note.

"I am sorry to see you leave us, Miss Danvers. You are a lovely young woman and I'm sure you will do well wherever you go." He bowed and offered a slight smile.

Tears threatened again at his kind words, but before she turned into a watering pot, she handed him the note for her landlady. "Please give this to Mrs. Ponsoby."

"Of course."

Lottie nodded and left the building. As much as she hated to do it, her next stop was the bank so she could withdraw the funds from the checks Mama had sent each month.

She had no idea where she would go, but definitely somewhere as far away from London and Bath as she could. Most likely France. There was little reason to believe anyone there would know Mrs. Danforth. In the small village close to her school, Mama was known as Mrs. Danvers, the loving and devoted mother to Miss Charlotte Danvers.

"Sir, you have a very persistent Lord Berkshire demanding to see you despite it being an improper time for making calls." Carter's butler, Manfred, was abruptly shoved aside by Grayson who barreled into Carter's bedchamber while he was still in bed.

"What the devil is going on?" Carter threw the covers off and grabbed his banyan, shrugging into it as he viewed Grayson with curiosity. "Has Bath been invaded?"

Grayson ran his fingers through his hair. "No. But you must dress quickly and meet my wife downstairs in your drawing room."

"Meet your wife? What is this about, Berkshire?" He slipped off the banyan and took the shirt his valet handed him.

"Lottie."

Before Carter could react, Berkshire was gone, and Carter was left staring at the closed door.

Lottie? It must be something serious for them to arrive at his house and drag him from his bed. Had Lottie been injured? His heart began to thump, knowing whatever Lady Berkshire planned to say to him was not going to be good news.

He grew frustrated with Manfred's attention to his ascot and bushed his hand away and left the room. He passed a footman as he came down the stairs. "See that my carriage is made ready to go."

"Yes, sir."

Whatever the problem was, he was certain to need his carriage. When he arrived at the drawing room, he found Lady Berkshire sitting on a chair, twisting a handkerchief in her fingers. Berkshire paced the room, looking as unsettled as his wife.

"What has happened? Is Miss Danvers ill?" He looked back and forth between the couple.

Lady Berkshire jumped up. "Oh, thank goodness you were quick. No, she is not ill, but you must stop her."

Since he knew Miss Danvers was in good health, he relaxed somewhat, but was still on edge. "Stop her from what?"

"Leaving Bath," Lady Berkshire said right before she burst into tears.

"Leaving?" His initial panic returned as he looked over at Berkshire. "Why is she leaving? Where is she going?"

"I think we should all sit down and discuss this calmly."

Carter felt anything by calm, but the only way he would get information out of Berkshire was to take a deep breath and listen.

Once they were seated, Carter looked over at Lady Berkshire. "Please explain to me what has happened and why Lottie is leaving Bath."

Lady Berkshire patted her swollen, red eyes. "Lady Pamela and I always knew Lottie was hiding something. She only spoke briefly of her past, merely telling us she had a mother in London from whom she was estranged."

Carter jumped in. "I knew she was hiding something because she attempted to disguise herself in London."

Lady Berkshire nodded. "Yes, the spectacles. Lottie only found out about a year ago—right before she moved to Bath—that her mother is a well-known . . ." Lady Berkshire looked in her husband's direction.

Berkshire cleared this throat. "Lottie's mother is Mrs. Danforth."

Carter blew out a low whistle. "*The* Mrs. Danforth?"

"You know her, too?" Lady Berkshire's distressed had returned.

"No. I don't know her, but I know of her. Most young gentlemen in London do. But from what I know, she only has one protector at a time and her current one has been with her for years. Much to many men's sorrow." Carter faced Berkshire. "I hope you don't mind me speaking so directly to your wife."

"Not at all. If we're going to help the girl, we need to have it all out in the open."

Lady Berkshire began to twist her handkerchief again. "Lottie came to me yesterday, very upset. Lord Sterling approached her while she was out with one of her students."

Carter felt his anger rise. "That cad has been insisting he knows her. He has upset her before with his insinuations and annoyance."

"Yes. Well, he apparently figured out why she looked familiar and asked her to consider going under his protection."

The heavy silence was broken by Carter's softly spoken words, "I will kill him."

Berkshire nodded. "However, there is a much more important matter you need to deal with."

"Then I can kill him?"

Lady Berkshire shook her head in annoyance. "Men! What you need to do right now is stop Lottie from leaving."

His blood was coursing so quickly through his body his head was pounding and felt as though it would explode. But dealing with Sterling would have to wait until he had Lottie firmly in his arms. "Of course, she wants to leave. Sterling has made it impossible for her to earn a living. No member of the *ton* will allow her to instruct their daughter."

Lady Berkshire nodded. "She was planning on packing up her flat and leaving today for I don't know where. She didn't even know herself."

"Today!"

"Yes. You must stop her," Lady Berkshire wailed.

"Anywhere she would go she'd have to start at the Bath Rail Station." Carter strode to the front door. "Where is my carriage?"

Manfred said, "Waiting for you, sir."

Carter took Lady Berkshire's hand in his. "You are a good friend. She will need you in the coming weeks."

"I love Lottie. I will always stand by her, have no doubt about that. Today I will visit with Lady Pamela and tell her what's going on. She will be there for Lottie, as well." Lady Berkshire touched Carter on his arm, the soft contact helping to calm him.

Carter examined Lady Berkshire's distressed face and turned to her husband. "Send for tea if you wish. I will fetch Miss Danvers. She is going nowhere. Trust me." With those words, he left the house and hopped into his carriage. "Bath Rail Station. Quickly."

He thought of a hundred different ways to approach Lottie, but only one remained in his mind. She was his. She would always be his, and no amount of reluctance from her because of her background would matter.

Now he understood her anxiety while they were in London. Anyone who had attended one of Mrs. Danforth's numerous parties would recognize Lottie. Although he'd never met Mrs. Danforth, Sterling's insistence that she looked familiar meant there must be a resemblance between the two women.

Mrs. Danforth was well known for her parties, but from what he'd heard they were far from hedonistic. The people who attend were from the demimonde, but there are also many members of the *ton*—gentlemen and a few ladies who were more daring, also graced her parlor, along with many from the wealthy merchant class.

She'd been known to have men thrown from her events for over-imbibing or harassing her female employees. In all ways, Mrs. Danforth was a very well-educated woman with excellent taste and a pleasing personality.

The Bath Station was crowded, as always. He searched the entire place, the waiting room, the ticket room, the benches crowded with travelers. He apologized numerous times for bumping into people. Frustrated, he was about to join the queue to ask the ticket seller if he remembered Lottie, when the door to the ladies' water closet opened and Lottie stepped out.

His heart stuttered. She was so beautiful, and she looked so lost and vulnerable. Everything protective in him rose up. He wanted to take her into his arms and hold her close. Tell her nothing bad would ever happen to her.

Slowly, he meandered through the throng and made his way toward her. She looked up and gasped when she spotted him. She turned quickly and tried to run into the station waiting room, but two women blocked the entrance and he caught up to her.

"Let me go. Please." Tears stood in her beautiful eyes.

"No, Lottie. I will not let you go. Not now, not ever." He wrapped his arms around her despite them being in the middle of the platform with bustling porters and passengers filling the space.

"You don't understand." Her voice was almost a moan.

He gripped her chin and tilted her face up. "Yes. I do. I understand and you must know by now that you belong to me."

"I don't want a protector!" She shoved against him and turned to flee, but he stopped her. "No, sweetheart. Please. I would never humiliate you in that way."

She stopped, one lone tear traveling down her soft skin. "Then I don't understand." She hiccupped, and he wanted to wrap her up and take her far, far, away. Away from a world that blamed her for something she had nothing to do with.

He smiled softly at her and cupped her cheeks. "I love you, Miss Charlotte Danvers. I want to make you my wife."

10

Lottie stared at Carter for a full minute, while her heart thundered in her chest and she repeated his words over and over in her head.

"I want to make you my wife."

Either she had developed a hearing problem or Carter did not fully understand her dilemma. Too confused to even think about what he said, she asked, "Why are you here?"

A frown was his only answer.

"I mean, here at the rail station."

He took her by the arm and moved her away from the noisy platform. "I will be happy to explain, but we must talk, and this is not the proper place for what I need to say."

She waved her ticket in his face. "I am leaving on the next train to London."

"You hate London, and you are going nowhere until I have the opportunity to say what I need to."

She could think of only one reason why he would be here and made that ridiculous statement. Addie. She must have told him about her encounter with Lord Sterling. Most likely Carter was here to play the part of a knight rescuing a lady in distress and talk her out of leaving. Even resorting to saying absurd things.

I want to make you my wife.

"My carriage is around the corner. Since I prefer privacy that is perfect." The determination on his face was almost comical.

She attempted to drag her feet. "I only have another twenty minutes until my train leaves."

He didn't answer her but continued to move her forward. "What I have to discuss will only take a few minutes."

Resigned to allowing Carter to have his say, she walked with him to his carriage. He helped her in, then joined her. Once they were settled, he tapped on the ceiling of the carriage and it moved forward.

"I thought this would not take long. I have a train to catch."

"No train. No leaving." He reached over and pulled her across the space until she was sitting on his lap.

"Mr. Westbrooke! This is most improper." For as inappropriate as it was, she couldn't stop the tingle inside that always taunted her when she was near him. The familiar scent of his bath soap and the solid muscles of his thighs that she felt right through their multiple layers of clothes teased her with things she could never have.

He wrapped his arms around her, pulling her close to him. "I would get down on one knee, but I'm afraid if I let you go you will foolishly jump from the moving carriage and hurt yourself."

She shook her head. "Please don't repeat what you said at the rail station."

"I will repeat it, and I meant it. I want you to be my wife. I want to be your husband. I want us to be married. To each other. You and me." He grinned. "Is that clear enough?"

Lottie groaned and closed her eyes. "I know why you're

doing this." She glared at him. "Addie must have told you about my encounter with Lord Sterling yesterday. She also told you I was leaving Bath to avoid the nastiness that would begin as soon as word spread who my mother is."

He continued to smile at her like she was telling him a lovely bedtime story. "Yes. Lady Berkshire was thoughtful enough to rouse me first thing this morning to tell me what happened with you and Sterling—who I will visit sometime soon for a chat—and your intention to leave Bath."

He held up his hand as she started to speak. "I don't personally know, but have heard of, Mrs. Danforth. What I didn't know was she had a wonderful, beautiful, smart, charming daughter." He cupped her cheeks. "Who I have fallen madly in love with."

She shook her head. "No. No. No."

"Yes." He shifted her so they sat face to face. "I don't care who your mother is. I love you. I want you to be mine."

She rested her hands on his shoulders. "You're the son of an earl! Can you imagine what your father would say if you were foolish enough to marry me?"

"I hope he would say 'congratulations' but even if he doesn't it makes no difference to me. He doesn't make me as happy as you do. He doesn't fill the open spots in my heart like you do."

She raised her eyes to the heavens. "Do you understand the sort of remarks that will be tossed my way? How you will be shunned for being married to me?"

He stiffened and the look on his face frightened her. "If *anyone* says *anything* to you in *any way* derogatory, they had better be prepared to be pummeled into the dirt."

"Then *you* had better be ready to spend quite a bit of money on bandages because once it becomes known that I am the daughter of Mrs. Danforth there will be plenty to say."

He ran his finger down her cheek, most likely attempting to distract her. "Please say yes. You will have the protection of my name. Of my family. No one will cast a slur upon you." He grinned again. "Even if they don't mind the threat of a beating."

If she seriously considered his offer—was she really thinking that way?—she had to tell him one more thing. "There is something else that you should know before you continue to wish me upon you for the rest of your life."

"Yes," he gently kissed her lips.

"I do not wish to . . ."

"To what?" He nibbled on her ear. 'Twas most distracting.

"To do what my mother does."

His eyebrows almost reached his hairline. "Become a courtesan?"

"No, of course not. I mean, yes, I don't want to be a courtesan. You're mixing me all up."

He took her hands in his and kissed her knuckles. "Just say it, sweetheart. Tell me what troubles you."

"I would not want to consummate our marriage."

CARTER STOPPED AND LOOKED UP AT HER FROM WHERE HE WAS about to kiss her knuckles again. "What?"

"I don't think I can do it." Her face was a bright red and she chewed on her lower lip. "I can't bring myself to do what my mother does for money."

"Then I won't pay you."

She pulled her hands away and placed them on her hips, which given the rough road they were traveling over, might end up with her on the floor. "This is not a joke."

"I'm not joking. I will do whatever it is you want me to do to make you feel secure and safe. But—I must draw the line at no consummation. For one thing, I would like children one day."

"I would too."

Carter shook his head, not believing the conversation they were having, but glad that it was taking long enough for her train to leave without her. "My love, in order to have children, there must be a man and a woman, and they must have sexual relations. And since it is quite rare for a woman to conceive with only one attempt, sexual relations must be continuous."

Carter was not discouraged. The time he'd kissed Lottie and when he'd held her in his arms while dancing, he sensed the unleashed passion in her. It might be something she thought she didn't want right now, but given enough time and effort, he knew he could convince her that pleasure between a husband and wife could be a wonderful thing.

"Just promise me that you will allow me to hold, touch, and kiss you."

"That's all?"

"For now."

She continued to study him, then slowly nodded. "Yes. If you are foolish enough to marry me with what you know about my mother and are willing to not push me on the other thing, then I will . . ."

"Marry me?"

"Marry you."

He immediately grabbed the train ticket out of her hand and tore it into pieces. "You will not be needing this."

"What will I do now? I've given up my flat, even though I still have a couple of weeks left on my rent."

Carter pulled her in for a kiss that quieted her. They could work out all the logistics and other problems she could imagine, but right now he wanted to kiss his betrothed.

She sat rigid at first, then as he continued the assault on

her mouth, she softened until she was plastered against him and moaning as he slipped into her mouth and tangled with her tongue. He placed his hand on her lower back and pulled her flush against his middle.

He pulled away and scattered kisses over her throat and jawline. "So soft." He pushed his fingers into her hair, knocking her hat off and causing numerous hairpins to go flying.

The woman who claimed she did not want to consummate their marriage was anything but reluctant and shy. She placed her hands on his cheeks and pulled him back to her lips.

The carriage slowed down due to traffic and she pulled back. "Wait!" She was panting and her cheeks were flushed. He saw the passion in her eyes and was quite satisfied with their arrangement. It would not take him long to seduce her into his bed.

"This is not proper. If someone were to look into the carriage I would be ruined." She bent to retrieve her hat and placed it on her head. He didn't have the heart to tell her that with the mess her hair was, the hat was not going to make a bit of difference in her appearance.

"You are correct. This is not the place for a betrothal celebration. Let me instruct my driver to proceed to Lord Berkshire's house. I am sure Lady Berkshire will be more than happy to house you until our wedding."

Lottie merely nodded and he tapped on the ceiling. The driver slid open the small door and looked down. "Yes, sir."

"Please proceed to Lord Berkshire's home."

"Very good, sir." The little opening slid closed and the driver picked up the pace, no longer under the previous instructions to wander the town aimlessly until Carter gave him other orders.

Lottie shifted off his lap, but he refused to let her move to the other side and instead anchored her against him.

She looked up at him, her lovely lips swollen from his kiss. "I don't want a wedding."

He grinned. She had agreed to marry him but didn't want to have sexual relations and didn't want a wedding. He was beginning to realize his soon-to-be wife could be adorably confusing at times. "Excuse me? Perhaps you mean no public wedding, my love?"

"Yes. No public wedding. Just us and witnesses."

"That is fine with me, but I must warn you I have no intention of waiting for banns to be called. I will have Berkshire apply to the Archbishop of Canterbury for a special license for us."

"What is that?"

"It will allow us to marry without the three weeks of calling banns. We can also be married anywhere, not necessarily in a church."

She closed her eyes and smiled. "That's perfect."

Carter took her hands in his. "Do you wish to discuss your mother with me?"

She immediately pulled away and crossed her arms over her middle. "No." She chewed on her lip for a minute, then said, "But I think since you are taking a chance on public denigration you have the right to know. Although, you must understand that I knew nothing of my mother's . . . occupation, until last year."

As much as he wanted to pull her back into his arms, he allowed her the free space that she evidently needed.

"Mama was a wonderful mother all my life. I spent my very early years with a lovely family in the country, the Stevens. They were an older couple with one grown son, and they all shamelessly doted on me. Mama said they were friends of hers and she wanted me to enjoy the country air. Since she needed to be in London, she preferred to have me live with them.

"She visited me quite often, bringing me presents and taking me out for what we called 'adventures.' That involved picnics, flower picking, even taking over Mrs. Stevens kitchen to bake bread, make jam from fruit we picked, and preparing one of Mama's favorites—pickled vegetables."

Carter immediately noticed the change in Lottie. The glow on her face and excitement in her eyes told him this break with her mother was probably slowly eating her away.

"Then when I turned ten years of age, she enrolled me in a private girls' boarding school outside of Paris. Amazingly enough, Mama made the trip to the school at least twice a month to visit with me. We had wonderful times then, also. We saw much of Paris, visited all the lovely tourist sites and ate delicious food."

Her voice slowly died away and she looked over at him. "Why would she do that? I just don't understand."

"When you learned of her situation, did you ask her why?" His heart was breaking at the look on her face. He had a feeling she had not told anyone all of this. Not even her best friends.

She shook her head. "No. I just ranted and yelled and acted very much like a child, I'm afraid."

"Then you left."

"Yes. That same night I hired a hackney and stayed in a hotel for two nights until I decided to come to Bath."

She rubbed her arms as if she had suddenly caught a chill. "I didn't have quite enough to set up a household with the money I had saved from my salary as a teacher the last two years at the school, so Mama gave me money to move, but I paid her back every penny."

He knew in his heart Lottie would never be at peace until she faced her mother once again. Right now, he was more concerned with getting her to Berkshire's house, applying for the special license and getting married.

A short wedding trip would give them time to separate themselves from any scandal that was starting in Bath. It would also provide him the opportunity to ease his wife into the marriage bed.

Always the optimist, he was certain it would all work out. What he wanted more than anything was to hear from Lottie's lips that she loved him as much as he loved her. It would take time, he was sure, but time was all he had once she was legally his.

"We have arrived, sweetheart." Carter pushed the curtain aside and looked out the window as they rolled to a stop in front of the Berkshire townhouse. The door to the carriage opened and he stepped out and turned to help Lottie down.

"Lottie! Oh, thank heavens he caught you in time." Lady Berkshire hurried down the steps, her arms out, ready to embrace her friend.

Both women were in tears as they hugged, and Carter grinned up at Berkshire who watched his wife with the same look of love, which Carter was certain was on his face, too.

11

LOTTIE ENTERED THE BREAKFAST ROOM AT BERKSHIRE townhouse to join Addie, Lord Berkshire, and Lady Pamela enjoying food that smelled wonderful.

"Pamela!" Lottie rushed forward as Pamela rose from her seat to embrace her.

Pamela hugged her tightly, then leaned back to look at her. "How d-dare you th-th-think you had to leave your h-home and fr-friends. Don't you know we all l-love you and will st-stand by you no m-matter what?"

Poor Pamela was in a frenzy for her stutter to be so bad when surrounded by friends. Lottie felt guilty for her friend's distress. She hugged her once again. "I know. I should have known better. But I was so . . ."

"Why don't you sit and have some breakfast?" Addie waved to the chair across from her. "I find, since my morning sickness has passed, I am ravenous all day. If this keeps up, I will hardly make it through the doorway when it's time for this child to be born."

Addie had told her the night before that she and Lord

Berkshire were expecting their first child in about five months. In her concern for Lottie the night she visited and told her she was leaving Bath, Addie had kept quiet about the baby because she didn't want to speak of her joy while Lottie was so upset.

"Isn't it w-wonderful, Lottie? We're g-going to be aunts!" Pamela beamed at Addie.

Lottie was indeed happy for Addie and Berkshire. At the same time, she thought it was quite brave of them to have another child when Berkshire's young son, Michael was deaf. Would this new baby have the same affliction?

Of course, if they engaged in the activity that married couples engaged in, another child was almost guaranteed.

That brought her thoughts back to her own situation. She'd spent a good part of the night tossing and turning, afraid that her feelings toward Carter were almost as strong as his toward her. Was it fair of her to marry him when he was sure to have some pain because of his choice?

Then she realized he was a grown man, knowledgeable of the world, and if he didn't care about her background, then she needed to stop worrying about it. She smiled thinking Carter's optimistic attitude toward life was rubbing off on her.

"Yes. That is exciting," Lottie said in answer to Pamela's question. "I plan to spoil the little darling shamelessly."

Pamela grinned at Lottie. "Except you might have one of your own one day."

"One certainly hopes so." Carter entered the dining room and walked over to Lottie, kissing her on the cheek. "Good morning, my love."

The fluttering in her stomach started up and she could feel the blush beginning in her toes and ending at her hairline. "Good morning, to you as well."

Addie and Pamela exchanged amused glances, which only deepened her blush.

Lottie reached for the platter of eggs in the middle of the table and placed one on her plate, along with a slice of toast and stewed tomatoes.

Carter and Berkshire became involved in a conversation about one of their business ventures, which helped Lottie to calm down and eat her breakfast.

"We must go shopping for a new dress for your wedding." Addie took her last sip of tea and placed the cup on the saucer.

"Yes. You d-definitely need a new dress." Pamela's eyes shone with excitement. It didn't appear that she felt left out, with one of her friends married and expecting a baby and her other friend getting ready for her wedding. After all, they had all promised each other that they were not considering marriage any longer and wanted the freedom of independent lives.

With Pamela's beauty and talent, Lottie never understood why she remained single so long. Of course, her stutter and crippling shyness didn't help, but she was a smart, witty woman. Who sang like an angel.

"I believe as soon as you are through with breakfast, we should all go to Madame LeBlanc's shop and have her make something wonderful for you," Addie said.

Carter covered Lottie's hand with his. "There is no time for making dresses, my love. Once Berkshire gets the special license, I intend for us to be married right away."

"What's the hurry?" Addie asked.

Carter squeezed Lottie's hand. "With Lord Sterling being rejected, I have every reason to believe he will resort to nasti-ness and spread the word about Mrs. Danforth."

Lottie sucked in a breath, hearing her mother's name so

easily slip from Carter's lips. She quickly looked around the table. No one gasped or even reacted to his statement. Of course not, they were her friends. She had to keep reminding herself of that. In fact, she should have told Addie and Pamela about her mother a long time ago.

"We can still visit with Madame LeBlanc. She has several already made-up dresses, and some of them are really quite nice. I was in her shop only a week ago and was quite surprised with the amount and variety of offerings she has."

Now that Lottie didn't have to spend her money on moving to a new place, she had enough funds to buy something special for her wedding. She would take it from her own savings and put the money from Mama back in the bank. "Yes. That is a splendid idea."

Carter waved a piece of toast around. "Visit whatever shops you want and buy whatever you like and have the bills sent to me."

"No. I cannot do that." Lottie shook her head. "I have money to pay for a dress." She was starting to panic. This was real. She was going to be Carter's wife, and for the rest of her life she would be under his control. Funny, how she'd never thought about that very much. She'd been so focused on not marrying at all that she never gave too much attention to the fact that her entire life was about to change.

"My dear, you are my betrothed, and soon to be my wife. I am legally and morally responsible for your lodging, food, clothing, and whatever else you want. Redecorate our home, throw out the furniture and buy new if that is what you want. 'Tis not just a requirement, but something I would love doing."

"Of course, Lottie. Mr. Westbrooke is right." Addie smiled gently at her; maybe afraid Lottie would again refuse. Or perhaps sensing the anxiety the conversation was having on her friend.

"I think at this point we can all drop the 'Lord' this and 'Lady' that and begin to use our given names." Lord Berkshire looked around the table. "'Tis quite awkward to call my wife's best friends Mrs. Westbrooke and Lady Pamela."

Everyone nodded their agreement.

"We must be off." After eyeing Lottie's plate, Addie stood and pushed her chair back. "There are numerous places we need to visit to get everything you will need for your wedding." She winked at Lottie. "And your wedding night."

Again, Lottie blushed to the roots of her hair. She noticed a slight smile on Carter's face, which she returned. She'd gone from suggesting they not consummate their marriage to eager anticipation of more of those feelings she'd experienced when Carter kissed her.

Addie bent to kiss Berkshire—or as he wanted to be known, Grayson—on the top of his head. Feeling giddy and foolish, Lottie did the same to Carter. It felt good, actually.

The three of them left the house and entered the Berkshire's carriage, which waited for them outside. Shopping for clothes while she didn't have to count pennies would be nice for a change.

Pamela looked over at Lottie as the carriage rolled forward. "Lottie, I don't want to upset you, but Addie preferred not to tell me about your mother and what the problem is. She said it would be your place to share that if you wanted to."

Lottie thought for a minute. "Since soon everyone in Bath will know, there is no reason for me to not tell you the entire story."

"I would like more information myself if you feel comfortable." Addie eyed her with concern. "We certainly don't want to spoil the fun of the day, but I think once everything is out in the open you will feel better."

"You are probably right. I felt a great deal of relief once Carter and I had a conversation about what to expect from those who will likely cause trouble."

It took the rest of the trip from Berkshire townhouse to the center of Bath, where the stores were they intended to visit, for Lottie to tell her best friends the story of why she had ended up in Bath and why she hid the information from them.

Addie was right. She felt much better once the carriage rolled up to Madame LeBlanc's shop and the three of them hurried to the door, arms linked, excited and chatting about a day of shopping.

"I KNOW YOU PLAN ON PAYING A CALL ON STERLING, WHICH IS exactly what I would do if it were Addie who had been subjected to the man's outrageous behavior. Shall I go with you to prevent you from conducting your wedding in a jail cell?"

"No. This is something I need to do myself. I can assure you I will remain in control and not kill the man." Carter winked and left the dining room. "I think."

Since Sterling was one of the indulged nobility who lived off a tidy inheritance, which he was no doubt going through with eagerness, the man would most likely be in one of his clubs.

Carter searched The People's Club on Harrington Place and The Bath and Country Club at 21-22 Queens Square to no avail. He also tried a few of the lesser-known and newer clubs without any success.

After a check of the Pump Room did not uncover the scoundrel, Carter directed his carriage driver to Sterling's house on Woodland Place, assuming the wastrel was sleeping off a night's revelry.

It took the butler a few minutes to answer the door once Carter dropped the knocker. The man was tall, old enough to be Sterling's great-grandfather and half asleep, his eyes bleary and his hair standing on end. "Yes?"

If this was the condition of the help, Carter imagined Sterling did not run the most organized and efficient household. "I am here to see Lord Sterling."

The man stood for a full minute just staring at him. About to lose his patience, Carter said, "May I come in and you fetch your master?"

"His lordship never rises before two o'clock in the afternoon."

"Today it will be different. Either you wake *his lordship* up or I will find him and do it myself."

"This is most improper." The man was having such a hard time standing up, Carter finally realized he was in his cups.

"Never mind." Carter nudged the man aside and entered the house. The rooms on either side of the entrance hall were littered with playing cards, empty glasses, several liquor bottles, and a few pairs of ladies' fancy drawers.

A table was turned upside down with a man curled up on it, clutching an empty bottle, snoring loudly.

It didn't take Carter long to assess what had happened the night before. Shaking his head in disgust, he climbed the stairs. "Sterling!"

He began opening doors, waking several guests, most of them naked, with more than one bed filled with multiple people.

"Sterling!"

Carter began pounding on doors until finally a woman

came out of one door, tying a belt around a man's banyan. "Who are you? What do you want?"

"I want Sterling." Carter jerked his head toward where she stood. "Is he in there?"

She yawned rather loud. A true lady. "Yes. But he's sleeping."

"Not anymore." He gently picked the woman up by her elbows and set her aside. "Go make coffee. Strong."

"I am not a servant!" She gasped.

"Then find one." He entered the room and closed the door. The curtains around the bed were closed and the drapes on the windows drawn.

"Time to rise, Sterling." Carter pulled back the drapes, allowing the bright sunlight to flood the room. Then he pulled the bed curtains back and stared at the lump of wasted human sprawled on the bed. Naked and smelling like a distillery.

He gripped Sterling's hair and pulled back so he could see his face. "Time to get up, Sterling."

Sterling's eyes opened and he groaned. "You must be a bad dream."

"No. I am your worst nightmare." Carter let go of the man's hair and walked to the dresser across the room. He picked up the half-full pitcher of water and dumped it on Sterling's head.

"What the blasted hell!" Sterling jumped up and shook his head, water splattering in every direction. "Is that you, Westbrooke? What are you doing in my bedchamber? Were you a guest last night? I don't remember." He groaned and held his head.

"Yes. It is I, Mr. Carter Westbrooke. I have come to deliver a message to you that I expect will take some repeating before it enters your soused brain."

"Is this about that whore?"

Carter's fist flew, connecting with Sterling's jaw. The man went down like a sack of flour.

"That was your second mistake."

Sterling eyed him from his bed. "Get out of my house."

Carter rubbed his knuckles, anxious to deliver another blow to the man. "In case you were wondering what your first mistake was, it was accosting my betrothed on a public street and insulting her with an offer that doesn't bear repeating."

"Your betrothed? Are you crazy man? She's—"

Carter wrapped his hand around Sterling's neck and pulled him forward, punching him in his soft middle. "Never. Say. That. Word. Again."

Sterling doubled over and looked up at him. "Do you know about her mother?" He raised his hand up. "Don't hit me again, or everything I drank last night will come up to greet us. I merely want to know if you are familiar with your future wife's family?"

"I know everything I need to know. But hear this, Sterling. If you so much as utter one single word about my wife, or her mother, or her aunts, sisters, cousins, or ancestors I will come back for you and I can assure you it won't be pleasant."

Sterling straightened and stood long enough to collapse on his bed. He regarded Carter with amazement. "You love her."

"Just remember what I told you. If anyone offers an opinion to you about Miss Danvers, or solicits your opinion, you will say nothing except flattering things about her. You are to become her champion. Is that understood?"

"I always thought love would do crazy things to a man, and here stands the proof." He raised his hand in surrender when Carter took one step toward him. "I agree. I will say nothing disparaging about the lady. If I meet her on the streets, or in a shop, or in church, I will treat her with the utmost respect."

Carter placed his hands on his hips. "From what I saw downstairs, and the condition you are in, it might do you some good to go to church."

With those words, he turned and pulled open the door. The woman who'd first approached him fell to the floor, obviously having had her ear pressed against the door. He pointed his finger at her. "Everything I said to him goes for you, as well."

12

LOTTIE ATTEMPTED TO FINISH BUTTONING HER WEDDING DRESS to no avail with her ice-cold and shaky hands. "Pamela, help, please."

Pamela moved away from the mirror where she was attempting to wrestle her curls into a decent chignon and held her hands out. She swatted Lottie's hands away. "Let me do this. You are making a mess of things." She shook her head. "Nervous brides."

Yes. Lottie agreed completely. The special license had arrived two days ago, and this morning was her wedding. She spent time last night making up two lists. One list for all the reasons she should not marry Carter. Or anyone else for that matter.

The second list was why she should marry Carter. Even though that one had just one entry, compared to about ten of the other list, and probably more if she gave herself more time, it convinced her she was doing the right thing.

He loves me and I'm quite sure I love him.

That was really all she needed to consider. Still, the doubts crept into her mind as she dressed.

Her thoughts then wandered to Addie's wedding and how Addie and her mother embraced and shared a few tears when Mrs. Mallory had seen her daughter as a bride for the first time.

She, who was so close to her mama all her life, was about to get married and she wouldn't be there. Didn't even know. Tears welled up in her eyes and she had a sudden need to throw herself on her bed like a young girl and cry her heart out.

Without a doubt, Lottie knew Mama would be thrilled to see her daughter marry. Especially to such an upstanding and honorable man.

Another sticking point was the lack of Carter's family at the wedding. She did ask him to have a small wedding with just them and their witnesses, but he agreed so readily she wondered if he wasn't relieved to not tell his family about her until after the deed was done.

So many things to worry about when she should be enjoying her day as a bride!

"I don't know what is going through your brain right now Lottie, but it must stop." Pamela finished with the long line of buttons and placed her hands on Lottie's shoulders and gave them a light squeeze. "Stop."

"Stop what?"

"Whatever it is you are telling yourself that is making you anything but a happy bride. Carter loves you. He has no qualms about marrying you, so you should trust him. You do trust him, don't you?"

"Yes. But . . ."

"No buts. Let's fix your lovely hat and then you will be ready to meet your groom."

The wedding was to be held in Carter's house with the vicar from their church officiating. Only Pamela, Grayson,

Addie, Grayson's son, Michael, and Michael's governess would be in attendance. While it was precisely what Lottie had asked for, now it seemed lonely.

"Lottie, I said stop." Pamela glared at her. "Besides, your hat looks lovely and it's time to go downstairs."

Lottie shook her head. "No. I don't think so."

Pamela's jaw dropped. "Why not?"

Lottie smirked at her friend. "Because you haven't finished with your hair and it's partially up and partially down."

Addie entered the room while Pamela was fixing her hair. "Sorry, we're late. I had to find time to eat breakfast." She stopped and looked at Lottie from head to toe. "You are stunningly beautiful, Lottie."

Lottie's eyes teared up again. "Thank you."

"What's wrong?" Addie walked up to her and raised her chin. "You should be glowingly happy."

"I am. But . . . my mother."

"Please don't start that again," Addie said as she sat on the bed. "This is a happy day for you."

"No. That's not what I meant. I'm thinking how lovely it was to have your mother there on your wedding day." She looked back and forth between Addie and Pamela. "Should I have invited her?"

The silence that followed was deafening. "Do you think you should have invited her?" Pamela asked.

"No. Yes. Oh, I don't know."

Apparently sensing a complete collapse of the bride, Addie jumped up and took Lottie's arm. "Time to go. Your groom awaits."

The three ladies descended the stairs and entered the drawing room. Lottie's breath caught when Carter turned from where he spoke to Grayson to look at her. The love in his eyes scared her to death, but at the same time warmed her and took away a lot of the worries that had been keeping her on edge since she'd agreed to his proposal.

Yes. This would all work out. Wouldn't it?

She accepted Carter's outstretched hand and moved next to him. The vicar began the ceremony, and it seemed within minutes they were declared husband and wife. Carter pulled her in for a very enthusiastic kiss, which had the vicar chuckling and the small gathering cheering.

"Please join my wife and I for breakfast," Carter said.

Lottie's stomach took a dip at *my wife*. It was done. She was his wife. He was her husband. For better or worse. Until death would they part. She glanced down at her wedding ring and thought back to the words Carter spoke when he placed the ring on her finger:

With this ring, I thee wed, with my body I thee worship, and with all my worldly goods I thee endow: In the name of the Father, and of the Son, and of the Holy Ghost. Amen.

She shivered and ran her palms up and down her arms.

"Are you chilly, sweetheart?" Carter viewed her with concern and she immediately relaxed. Maybe they hadn't known each other very long, but she knew in her heart that this man would always take care of her, would always stand by her side.

"Just a bit. A warm cup of tea will help."

The group gathered in the dining room where they enjoyed a feast of lobster salad, several chicken dishes, ham, green beans, and chicken consommé, with pastries and jellies and cream for dessert, along with the traditional wedding cake.

After a few hours of lively conversation, bantering, and teasing about the upcoming wedding night, the group broke up and left Carter and Lottie with wishes for a happy marriage and a few winks from Grayson about the one thing Lottie was growing apprehensive over.

Maybe sensing her mood, Carter pulled her in for a lovely kiss that relaxed her, but at the same time reminded her of what was to come. "Would you like to take a stroll to help digest all that wonderful food?"

Lottie hoped her sigh of relief was not too evident. She certainly didn't think Carter would drag her upstairs the minute the door closed on the last of their guests and toss her on the bed then jump on her. But the anticipation was making her skittish.

"Yes. I love the idea of a walk."

They shrugged into their coats and added gloves and hats. Lottie was amused when Carter took the scarf that hung on her coat and wrapped it around her neck, tucking it in. She could get used to that kind of treatment.

The air was crisp and cool, but soon spring weather would warm things up a bit. They enjoyed a leisurely stroll, going over the wedding breakfast and commenting on how Addie and Michael showed the group how sign language worked. It was truly fascinating.

After about a mile, Carter turned them and they headed back to his house. Actually, her house now, as well. The closer they grew to the dwelling, the more her stomach knotted.

"Relax, sweetheart. I am not going to drag you right to bed."

THE MINUTE CARTER TURNED THEM TOWARD HOME, HE FELT Lottie tense. The relaxed conversation they'd been enjoying came to an end and she seemed to have nothing further to say, even though she'd been quite chatty up until then.

"I'd like to share with you how I prefer to end my days." He pulled her closer, away from a man walking his very unfriendly looking dog.

"Yes. I would like to know that. It feels so odd to me not to be returning to my own flat."

Deciding to keep her talking as the best way to relax her, Carter asked, "And what sort of routine do you follow in the evenings?"

"Generally, I change out of my day clothes and get comfortable in my very warm and cozy robe. I like to have a glass of heated milk and then I read until my eyes turn bleary."

"Indeed? Very similar to my routine. Except it's not warm milk, but a small glass of smooth brandy. But I also read until I cannot see anymore."

"History?"

"Some. But I've also been known to read a novel or two."

Perhaps speaking about their nightly routines was the best way to relax his skittish wife, but for him it only reminded him of how his nightly routine was about to change, starting tonight. That thought brought excitement and a need to move a bit faster, but he kept his eagerness in check so as not to send his wife running in the opposite direction.

Once they arrived home, his butler, Milton, helped them out of their coats and hats. Carter had introduced Lottie to his meager staff. He only employed a housekeeper, butler, and cook. The housekeeper, Mrs. Davis, took care of the daily cleaning up and had a girl from town come in once a week to give the place a thorough cleaning and change the bed linens.

"It just occurred to me, Lottie. You might want to add staff. I only have the housekeeper, cook, and butler whom you've already met. Do you have a lady's maid?"

"Goodness, no. I made do by myself while I was employed at the school, and with my meager wages, there was no money for a lady's maid. Besides, most women no longer have lady's maids since clothing is somewhat easier to get into and out of."

She should not have mentioned getting out of her clothing. Blood raced to his groin area, causing him to adjust his trousers so as not to alarm his wife.

"Let us retire to the drawing room. Maybe open a bottle of wine to celebrate our wedding?"

Lottie agreed so eagerly he figured she saw that as a way to avoid the bedroom, or maybe even to drink enough to forget what she was doing. That he would not allow. Bedding a drunk woman was worse than not bedding one at all.

However, a little bit tipsy to relax her was a great idea. He sent Milton to the wine cellar and he and Lottie settled on the comfortable sofa in front of the fireplace. Normally he wouldn't have a fire going this far into the spring, but since Lottie shivered every once in a while, it was probably a good idea.

"I know I mentioned this before, but if you want to redecorate, please feel free to do so. Just pick out what you want and have the bills sent to me."

Lottie laughed as she took a sip of her wine. "I am afraid you may one day regret telling me to get what I want and have the bills sent to you. Remember I grew up in a school and the idea of a cozy home with things to my liking is quite tempting."

Carter took the glass from her hand and placed it on the table in front of them. He turned her toward him and tucked a loose curl behind her ear. "I can afford whatever it is you want. Make this home to your liking. You can do the same at our London townhouse."

"You are too generous."

"No. What good is money if one cannot do pleasurable

things for the people they love? I love you, Lottie, and I want you to be happy."

He hoped she would say the words back to him, but she apparently was not ready. However, he had no doubt he would hear them one day.

After the wine bottle had been emptied, and they were both relaxed and laughing at some silly thing that Grayson had said at the wedding breakfast, Carter took Lottie's hand in his. "Let us retire to the bedroom and get more comfortable."

Expecting to see Lottie resist, he was pleasantly surprised when she took his hand and stood. "Yes. I think that is a good idea."

He cupped her cheeks and slowly lowered his mouth to hers. "I want you very much, Mrs. Westbrooke." His lips met hers and he took her mouth in a possessive kiss. She was his, to love, care for and protect. He would give his life to keep her from harm and do anything to make her happy.

Carter scooped her into his arms and made for the staircase. Lottie pulled back and grinned at him. "You cannot think to carry me upstairs!"

"What? You think I'm not able to carry my wife up a few steps?" He gave her a quick kiss. "You underestimate me, sweetheart."

He raced up the stairs; both of them doubled over with laughter by the time he had made it to the bedroom, kicked the door shut, and tossed her onto the bed.

Carter joined her on the bed and bent his elbow, propping his head on his hand. "I must admit I am a bit out of breath." He grinned as he took the time to catch his breath. Perhaps he should spend some time at the boxing club.

He studied Lottie as she stared back at him. Her hair had fallen from the chignon she'd worn all day, leaving dark wavy curls resting on her shoulders, covering her breasts. Her beautiful mouth formed a soft smile as she reached up and pushed the hair from his forehead.

Wrapping his arm around her waist, he pulled her close until she fit snug against him, her curves aligning with his body perfectly. "You are so beautiful. Not just your looks, but your soul." He kissed her gently, twirling his finger in the soft, scented strands of her hair.

"Since you don't have a lady's maid, I will help you remove your dress." Before she could protest, he stood and pulled her up. He continued to kiss her as he unbuttoned the dress and slid it off her creamy shoulders.

Unable to help himself, he placed his lips on her warm skin, right where her neck met her shoulder. The scent of lavender and lemon drifted from her skin. "You smell wonderful."

"Your turn, now husband." Lottie undid his ascot and with his help removed his jacket, vest, and shirt. When he stood in only his trousers, stockings and shoes she stepped back. "I think I will let you do the rest." Then with a giggle, she dove for the bed and pulled the coverlet up to her chin, grinning at him.

"Wait a minute. You must remove the rest of your clothes."

"I think I'm quite comfortable as I am." She wore only her soft cotton knickers with lace trim and a corset.

"What about your stockings and shoes?"

Lottie laughed and shoved down the covers. "I forgot." She hopped up and quickly removed the half-boots. When she pushed the bottom of her knickers up and reached for the top of her stocking, she looked over at him and blushed. "Don't look."

Oh, he was certainly going to look, but not at the present time. He didn't want to break the playful mood his wife was in.

The wine had done its work. She was relaxed and giddy, and he loved it.

He pushed down his trousers but climbed into bed next to her with his drawers still on. He reached for her, pulling her into his arms. She was all soft, warm, and from the look on her face, willing.

He'd waited a long time for this, and he would take his time. Love her the way she should be loved and according to the vow he took:

With my body I thee worship

13

One week. They were married for one week. Lottie stood at the window in their bedchamber and watched the carriages go by and the servants hurrying from the shops back to their homes.

Everything looked so normal. But she was about to step off a cliff. At least that was how it felt. Carter had decided that once they returned from their brief wedding trip that they should immediately show themselves in town as a married couple.

His plans for the day included a ride through Royal Victoria Park, then a stroll through Milsom Street and the shops there, followed by luncheon at Sally Lunn's, then a short respite at home before they joined Grayson and Addie to tackle the theater crowd that evening.

Carter's theory was they must put themselves out there to squelch any sort of gossip or rumors that might have been started. He wanted to show the world that she was his and if anyone had the audacity to treat her in any way except honorable, they would deal with him.

As much as she loved the idea of him standing up for her,

she was terrified. Her protected life had never prepared her for facing down criticisms and disdain. But she knew in her heart that her husband was correct.

She heard him enter the room and immediately felt his warm breath on her neck where he nuzzled and kissed her. "Are you ready to face the world as Mrs. Westbrooke?"

She turned in his arms. "Maybe we should wait a few days."

"Ah. No, sweetheart. I know you're a strong woman. There is no need to wait, it will only get harder with each passing day." He took her hand. "Come, the carriage awaits."

The early spring weather allowed them to wear only light coats. Almost as if the weather wanted to encourage this jaunt, the sun shone, and there was nary a cloud in the sky.

The short ride in the open-air phaeton to Royal Victoria Park was filled with comments from Carter. Most likely to keep her from jumping from the vehicle and running home.

"There is an interesting story about Royal Victoria Park." He shifted his seat and turned toward her, still keeping his eye on the traffic. "When Queen Victoria was a mere eleven years, she dedicated the park. Shortly thereafter, a reporter wrote the story in a newspaper and disparaged her dress. Called her dowdy, or something like that.

"The future queen was so distressed that she never visited Bath again. One time she was on a train that traveled through Bath. She had all the shades in the windows in her car drawn so she would not have to look at the city when they passed through."

"My goodness. I take it she was not one to easily forgive."

Carter shook his head. "I guess not."

They entered the park and began their slow ride. Carter had picked a good time because there were some vehicles and strollers about, but the usual crowds who filled the park in the warmer weather were still most likely lounging in their beds.

Within a few minutes, however, they were approached by two carriages. Mrs. Silverstein and her daughter rode in one and nodded in their direction. The second carriage held Lady Edwards-Hughes, along with two other ladies Lottie didn't know.

Lady Edwards-Hughes waved them down. Carter placed his hand on hers resting in her lap. "Be at ease, sweetheart." He smiled at the ladies. "Good morning, ladies. Beautiful day for a ride, is it not?"

The second woman in the carriage, who apparently knew Carter looked him in the eye. "I understand you married recently, Mr. Westbrooke?"

"Yes. I did. In fact, allow me to present to you ladies my wife, Mrs. Westbrooke."

He turned to Lottie. "May I make known to you Lady Edwards-Hughes, Mrs. Edward Turner, and Mrs. Gregory Cooper."

Lottie already knew Lady Edwards-Hughes through one of her students but did not know the other two. She smiled and nodded her head. "Good morning, ladies. It is a pleasure to meet you."

The one who had been introduced as Mrs. Cooper raised a quizzing glass and stared at her. "Why don't I know you, gel? Are you from London?"

"No, ma'am. I live here in Bath."

She harrumphed. "You must have been hiding."

Although Lottie's heart was pounding, and she could feel the perspiration on her upper lip, so far none of the ladies either knew who she was or didn't care. That last part was highly unlikely since women were known to love the sound of a scandal.

"You must bring your lovely new wife to dinner one evening, Mr. Westbrooke. I will send a note around." Lady Edwards-Hughes tapped her driver with her parasol and the carriage moved forward.

Carter turned to her with a bright smile on his face. "That went rather well, wouldn't you say?"

Lottie followed the carriage with her eyes. "Yes. It did go well." She turned back to Carter. "Not that I am looking for trouble, but I have a feeling Lady Edwards-Hughes will 'forget' to send around a note. Once she makes known to her circle of friends who your new wife is, she will no doubt be told about my scandalous background."

Carter took in a deep breath as their carriage moved forward again. "Lottie you must stop this. You do not have a scandalous background. You have been nothing but a proper, upstanding, honorable young lady. You are not your mother."

They remained silent for the rest of the carriage ride, except for a few comments on the budding flowers. Carter took the carriage from the park to Milsom Street where they left it at a public mews and began their stroll.

They visited a few of the shops. Lottie bought a new hat and pair of gloves that Carter insisted she absolutely must have. She rather enjoyed purchasing things and not watching her money dwindle.

"I believe it is time for luncheon, my dear. Shall we proceed to Sally Lunn's?"

It was less than a ten-minute walk from the Milsom street shops to North Parade Passage where Sally Lunn's was located. Lottie was still on edge every time someone approached them and spoke with Carter, but so far no one screamed 'harlot' at her. Was it possible that no one in Bath really cared that the well-known solicitor and businessman, son of the Earl of

Huntingdon, and brother to the Viscount Hastings married the daughter of a courtesan?

As much as she would have loved to think that, she remained on guard.

"Westbrooke, come join us." A man waved to them as they entered the restaurant. He sat at a table big enough for six, but only two other men sat with him.

Lottie immediately stiffened and stopped in her tracks. "No. I don't think we should join them."

Carter wrapped his arm around her waist and moved her forward. "These are friends of mine from Harrow."

"Oh, no." She shook her head, feeling as though he was dragging her toward her death.

"They are nice men. You have nothing to worry about."

Lottie took a deep breath and allowed him to lead her to the table. The three men stood as they arrived. "Gentlemen, allow me to introduce you to my wife, Mrs. Lottie Westbrooke."

"Wife!" One of the men grinned in Carter's direction. "So you got caught in the parson's noose."

"Lottie, these reprobates are Mr. Collins, Mr. Wilkerson, and Lord Derby."

Her mouth dried as desert sand, Lottie merely nodded and smiled.

"I say, Mrs. Westbrooke, you look familiar." Lord Derby tilted his head, studying her.

Lottie glanced at Carter who squeezed her hand. "Lottie's mother is Mrs. Danforth."

All three men stared at her. "Yes. There is a strong resemblance," Mr. Collins said. Then he looked over at Carter. "You are a brave man, Carter."

Lottie felt as though she would faint and squeezed Carter's hand so hard, she was afraid she would break his bones. Then

Lord Derby picked up his cup and saluted them. "And a very lucky one, from what I can see. Best wishes to both of you."

The other two men picked up their cups as well and wished them happiness. And that was the end of the conversation about their marriage and her mother. Lottie was still shaken by the time their food arrived and only picked at the meal, still waiting for some lewd comment to be made.

But they all ate their meal, conversed about various subjects and parted ways.

Shortly after dinner two days after their foray into town, Carter sat at his desk in his office, going over his books. He'd been quite pleased by the response—or lack of response— they'd had with the people they'd met the last couple of days.

True to her word, Lady Edwards-Hughes sent around a note inviting him and Lottie to dinner the following week. As much of an optimist as he was, however, he still felt as though he were waiting for the next shoe to drop.

On Saturday, he planned to bring Lottie, along with Pamela, Addie, and Berkshire to the Assembly, and then church the next morning. He wanted to announce their marriage to one and all so Lottie would not fret all the time.

Milton tapped lightly on the door and opened at his bidding. "Sir, your brother, the Viscount Hastings has called."

Carter closed the book he'd been working on and stretched his cramped muscles. "Charles is here? Splendid! Show him in." His brother must have taken the last train from London, so he would make sure to have a room prepared for him.

Right behind Milton, Charles strode into the room. Carter was so happy to see his brother that he almost missed the derision on his face. Almost.

"What brings you here, Charles?" Carter waved to the comfortable chairs near the fireplace where they both settled.

Charles tugged on the cuffs of his jacket and leaned back, his foot resting on his bent knee. "I hear tell in London that my younger brother got married."

"You hear correctly. I hope you have come to wish me happy."

"Actually, dear brother, not exactly."

Carter felt the hairs on the back of his neck rise. "And why is that?"

Charles hopped up and leaned his arm on the fireplace mantle. "Because I am hoping I heard wrong. Did you or did you not marry Mrs. Danforth's daughter?"

The happiness at seeing his brother faded into rising anger. "I married a lovely woman named Miss Charlotte Danvers."

"Don't play with me, brother. Did you marry that whore's daughter?"

Carter rose slowly, his heart pounding and his fist anxious to do some pounding on his brother. "I said I married *Miss Charlotte Danvers*. Who her family members are has nothing to do with my wife."

"Are you out of your mind, Carter?" Charles began to pace. "Do you have any idea what being associated with her will do to the family name? Before you jumped into marriage with the chit did you think about that at all?"

Since Lottie was upstairs in the sitting room next to their bedchamber going over swatches of material for new drapes and bed coverings, the last thing he wanted to do was have her hear his brother. He walked over to the office door and closed it.

"Whom I choose to marry is my own business. When you and Lizzie got caught half undressed in Lord Munthorpe's library and had a hurry-up wedding, did I criticize you?"

Charles turned and placed his hands on his hips. "I did not marry a light-skirt."

Before he even had a chance to think about it, Carter swung his fist at his brother and sent him flying, landing on the sofa. "My wife is no light-skirt. She is a gently-reared woman, the product of an exclusive girls' school in France."

Charles rubbed his chin. "If you are so very proud of your wife, why did you not invite your family to the wedding? And when were you planning on telling Mother and Father? After the first child arrives in about six months?"

Carter leaped on his brother and they went down, knocking furniture out of the way. They rolled around on the floor, the sound of flesh hitting flesh reverberating throughout the room.

"Stop!" Lottie stood in the doorway, her hands on her hips, watching the two men in horror. "What is going on here?"

Carter gave his brother one last punch to the jaw before climbing to his feet. He wiped the blood streaming from his nose. "Lottie, go back upstairs. This doesn't concern you."

"Yes. It does," Charles said from his position on the floor.

"Would you mind introducing me to this gentleman you just engaged in fisticuffs with?" She walked farther into the room.

Apparently, Lottie missed the 'and obey' part of the marriage ceremony when the vicar said, 'love, honor, and obey.'

"I am the Viscount Hastings." Charles climbed to his feet and brushed his clothing off. "Your brother-in-law, I am sorry to say."

Carter leaped over the sofa, grabbed his brother by the throat and they both went down.

Lottie stamped her foot. "Stop this. Stop this now!" She ran to a small table and picked up a vase, holding it in the air. "I shall smash both of you on the head with this."

Carter rolled off his brother and stood. He stumbled over to Lottie. "Dear heart, please go back upstairs."

She shook her head. "No. I want to know what's going on in here. If this is your brother, why are you both rolling around on the floor, fighting like a couple of school boys?"

Charles tugged on his jacket sleeves and looked over at Carter. "Are you going to tell her, or do I have to?"

"Tell me what?" Lottie looked concerned, and Carter knew his brother was about to break her heart.

He tried once more. "Lottie, this is between us. Please forget what you saw and go back upstairs."

"You're starting to scare me," she said. She looked over at Charles. "Say what my husband is reluctant to have me hear."

"Fine. I will do this because I love my brother. I love my entire family and frankly, him marrying you will cause a great deal of harm to our name." He turned to Carter. "There. It's been said. I'm sorry, Miss Danvers, but that's what the situation is."

Lottie drew back as if she'd been slapped. "It's Mrs. Westbrooke," she muttered, then with her chin raised, made her way out of the room, closing the door softly behind her.

Carter turned on his brother. "Don't ever come to my house again. You are not welcomed. And if Mother and Father feel the same way, that goes for them as well. I love my wife. She is a wonderful, kind, caring, intelligent woman." He pushed Charles out of the way and made his way to the door. "You can see yourself out."

As expected, Lottie was sitting on the bed, staring at the wall. One lone tear tracked down her cheek. "I knew this would happen."

Carter sat next to her and took her hand. "My brother is a

nodcock. He was always a hot-headed youth and never thinks things through before he opens his mouth."

Lottie wiped her cheek and shook her head. "No. Your brother was correct. I told you before we married that your family name would be besmirched." She turned and smiled softly. "But I hate being right."

Carter wrapped his arms around her and held her tight. "You are not right. My brother doesn't matter. Everyone here in Bath has been more than pleasant to both of us. He lives in London. We never need to see him again."

"And the rest of your family. Will you write them off that quickly, as well?"

He tucked a curl behind her ear and cupped her chin. "You are my family now. We will have children and build a life for ourselves that we're happy with. We don't need anyone else."

Lottie closed her eyes and then pulled him in for a kiss that ended in an explosion of passion. They made love twice and finally fell into an exhausted sleep.

Carter awoke at dawn the next morning and reached over to pull Lottie to him. The space alongside him was empty. And cold. A search of the house proved it to be empty, as well.

His wife had left him.

14

CARTER POUNDED ON THE BERKSHIRE RESIDENCE'S FRONT DOOR. He didn't care if he woke the entire neighborhood. He was certain his wife had fled to Addie and he wanted, nay needed, to coax her back home.

His life was nothing without her. In the short time they'd been married, he knew that in his heart. Hell, he was prepared to move to France and spend the rest of his life there if that was what it took to make her comfortable.

He pounded once again, and the door was finally opened by Berkshire's butler. "Good morning Penrose. Is his lordship up and about yet?"

It was quite early, and Carter knew Berkshire would probably not be ready to receive company, but he was sure Lottie was here.

"I'm afraid not, sir. If you will wait in the drawing room I will see if he can receive you."

Carter nodded and began to pace in the room. What he wanted to do was run up to the bedchamber floor and open every door until he found his wife. But good manners prevailed, and he waited.

Within minutes Berkshire entered the room, tying the belt of his banyan. "What the devil is going on?"

"Where's my wife?"

Berkshire stared at him. "Your wife? How the devil should I know where she is? Can't you keep track of her?"

Carter frowned. "Are you sure she's not here?"

Berkshire ran his fingers through his hair. "I must admit I do not do an inventory of residents before I retire each night, but as far as I know she is not here."

"Can you call Addie down so I can speak with her?"

Berkshire's brows rose. "You think my wife is hiding your wife?" He shook his head and walked toward the door. "Too bad it's too early for a brandy."

About ten minutes later, Berkshire returned with Addie in tow. The woman must have come right from her bed since her hair was still down and she was wrapped in a dressing gown, a slight bulge in her middle. "What's this about Lottie being missing?"

Carter groaned at the sincerity in Addie's words. "She's not here?"

"No. What happened?"

"My arse of a brother came to my house last night and caused a ruckus about marrying Lottie. Unfortunately, he told her precisely why he was unhappy about the match. She was upset, but I thought she had calmed down. But this morning she was missing. I was sure she was here."

"Would she be at the train station again?" Addie said, covering her mouth with the back of her hand when she yawned.

"Honestly, I was so certain she was here I never thought of where else she could be. But that is a very good idea." Carter strode from the room. "If she does come here, don't let her leave and send someone to fetch me."

It seemed to take the carriage forever to go the short distance from the Berkshire residence to the Bath Rail Station. Carter hopped out before it came to a complete stop. He charged past the ticket booth, with the long queue waiting to buy tickets, after assessing each person.

The platform was bustling again, porters everywhere loading and unloading luggage. Families were hugging and kissing and waving goodbye.

"If you're looking for me so you can hit me again, here I am." Carter turned to see Charles standing in front of him. He had a split lip and a nasty black eye. Carter hadn't bothered to even look in a mirror to assess the damage his brother had done to him. He assumed he looked the same.

"Get out of my way." Carter pushed Charles aside and continued his search.

"Wait." Charles grabbed his arm. "I want to apologize for what I said to your wife yesterday."

"Oh, do you now? How very nice. Unfortunately, my wife has disappeared." Carter tapped his finger against his lips, tramping down the anger that was slowly building. The last thing he needed to do was get into another fight with his brother and end up in jail. "I wonder if what you said to her had anything to do with it?"

"Do you think she's here?" Charles looked around the throng.

"No. I don't think she's here. That's why I'm frantically looking around this blasted train station for her." He gave his brother another shove. "Now, get out of my way."

"I want to help."

Carter looked, really looked at his brother. The man was a mess. Not only did he show the results of their altercation, but guilt was written all over his face, as well as signs of a night of dissipation. But with Lottie missing, he had no time for sympathy for Charles. "No. I don't need your help." With those words, he walked off and continued his search.

After about an hour, Carter resigned himself to the fact that either Lottie had left on an earlier train, or she wasn't here at all. He saw no more of his brother and left the station.

On the ride home he considered everything again, and then realized he'd overlooked one thing. He tapped on the carriage ceiling.

"Yes, sir."

"Instead of home, take me back to Berkshire's townhouse."

His driver turned the carriage and headed in that direction. When they arrived, Carter jumped from the vehicle and once more pounded on the front door.

"Yes, Mr. Westbrooke." Penrose offered him a slight smile. "Before you ask, his lordship and ladyship are in the breakfast room. Please feel free to join them."

"Thank you." Carter strode down the corridor to the breakfast room where he found both Berkshire and Addie having breakfast.

"She wasn't at the rail station." Carter slumped in the chair across from Addie.

"Why don't you have some breakfast and we can discuss this." Addie narrowed her eyes at him. "You look awful. You have a bruise on your cheek and jaw."

Carter waved his hand. "No matter. I've come to ask you to either accompany me or give me the address of Lady Pamela."

Addie's brows rose. "You think she's there?"

"I'm praying she's there. If she isn't, I have no idea where else to look."

Berkshire wiped his mouth with his napkin. "You don't suppose she's returned to France, do you? It seems that was the only place the poor girl felt safe and secure."

Carter nodded. "A good point. But let's hope she's right here in Bath at Pamela's home."

Addie pushed her chair back and Berkshire jumped up to help her up. Despite what he was going through Carter had to laugh at how doting Berkshire was with his wife. By the time the babe grew close to arrival, he would probably be carrying her everywhere.

"I will go with you. Just give me a minute to freshen up." Addie walked past him and rested her hand on his shoulder. "We'll find her. She loves you; you know."

"Yes. I have surmised. But that doesn't do me any good if I can't find her."

Addie squeezed his shoulder. "We will."

LOTTIE ROLLED OVER AND FELL ONTO THE FLOOR, FORGETTING she was sleeping in Pamela's sofa and not her own comfortable, large bed. "Ouch." She rubbed her shoulder and climbed back up.

"Do you feel any better?" Pamela sat on a chair across from the sofa.

"No." Lottie grinned. "But I didn't expect to, anyway." She had arrived at Pamela's room in the boarding house around six in the morning after a night of tossing and turning and finally deciding she had to set Carter free. He didn't know what was best for him, so she had to be the strong one and do it.

They made love twice, and Lottie had relished every minute, knowing it would be their last. She left Carter sleeping soundly, sprawled across the bed, his face bruised from the beating he'd taken from his brother. From what she'd seen, Charles must look much the same way.

"What are you going to do?" Pamela eyed her with sympathy. "You know Carter loves you very much. Do you really think he will give you up because his brother doesn't approve?"

Lottie had told Pamela what happened when she showed up at the boarding house's front door after a quick hackney ride from her home. Rather than offer advice, Pamela was smart enough to just listen to Lottie's sad tale. Then she brought out a pillow and blanket and invited her to sleep for a few hours. Which she apparently had done.

"Would you like some breakfast?"

"No. I have no appetite, but a cup of tea would be nice." Lottie looked down at her dress, a wrinkled mess. "I didn't even bring any clothes with me. I was afraid of waking Carter up and rehashing what happened last night."

"I hope you plan on talking to him before you make any major decisions. He has the right to let you know how he feels."

Lottie snorted. "I know how he feels, but he's not thinking clearly. We're talking about the rest of our lives, Pamela. I can't have his entire family under a cloud of disgrace because of me."

Pamela moved across the room and sat next to Lottie, putting her arm around her shoulders. "Your husband is a grown man. He knows what he can handle and what he cannot. Just give him a chance to talk to you before you do anything rash."

Lottie sighed. It was such a dilemma. She had spent a good part of the night before replaying Charles's words in her mind and cringing each time.

They were in the middle of tea when a knock sounded at the bedroom door. "I am sure I know who that is," Pamela said as she stood to answer the door. She turned to Lottie. "Do not try to climb out a window. This is the second floor."

"My lady, your guest has a caller." The man who manned

the front door peeked around Pamela. "She must come downstairs to the drawing room to meet with him."

Pamela turned. "Won't you at least talk to him?"

Lottie climbed to her feet. "Yes. I might as well get this over with."

As she entered the small drawing room next to the front entrance hall, Carter turned from where he stood in front of the window. "Lottie!" He strode across the room and pulled her to him, wrapping his arms around her. "What the devil did you do this for? I've been frantic, looking for you all morning." He leaned back and placed his hands on her shoulders. "Don't ever do this to me again."

Pamela entered the room, shrugging into her coat. "I am going for a walk. The fresh air will do me good." She winked at Lottie and left.

"Would you like some tea?" Lottie asked after the front door closed.

"Tea? I need a nice strong, large glass of brandy. You scared me to death."

Lottie took his hand and led him to the sofa in the drawing room. "I'm sorry. I didn't mean to scare you, but I have to make plans and I would not be able to do that with you there."

"Plans?" He cupped her chin and kissed her, taking complete possession of her mouth. Tears rushed to her closed eyes, knowing in her heart this was to be one of the last kisses she would ever share with Carter.

Lottie pulled back first and placed her hand on his chest. "Please let me have my say."

Carter crossed his arms over his chest, certainly not in a way that suggested he was ready to listen to her. "Go on. Then I will have my say."

Lottie stood and backed away, not wanting to be too near him. Already her resolve was fading with him merely kissing her once and sitting there watching her. How her heart ached. If only she had used her common sense and refused to marry him.

"Please don't blame your brother for this."

Carter snorted. "Yes. That seems like something I would consider. He's dead to me, Lottie."

She shook her head furiously. "No! That's precisely why I want to have this talk. He's your brother."

"Half-brother."

She frowned. "What?"

Carter uncrossed his arms and stood, but when she backed up, he stayed where he was. He rotated his neck, placed his hands on his hips, and then said, "You were not the only one with secrets, my dear. Many years ago, my mother and father were separated for a short while. I never learned what the cause was for the separation, but during that time my mother had a very brief affair."

If Carter had told her his mother had been an opera singer in her youth, she would not have been more surprised. "An affair?"

"As I said. Very brief. But during that time she became pregnant. With me."

Lottie collapsed onto the sofa, her mouth agape. "You are not the Earl of Huntingdon's son?"

"As far as the world is concerned, I am the Earl of Huntingdon's third son. But in reality, you could almost say I was a bastard since my parents were not married to each other."

She shook her head as if to clear it. "Does your father—er, the Earl—know?"

"Yes. Once I became old enough to understand, my mother told me. She and my father—the Earl—sat side by side on the sofa and told me this. He had forgiven her when she returned to him and always considered me his son."

"So, Charles—"

"—Is my half-brother."

Lottie was stunned. Here she thought she brought disgrace to his family, and yet his mother had made one mistake and her husband took her back. "How do they get along now?"

Carter laughed. "They are devoted to each other. In fact, one time Father told me that what happened between them, and his acceptance of her mistake and my arrival, put their marriage on stronger ground."

"Your father is an amazing man." She thought for a minute. "Did your mother ever tell you who your real father is?"

"Lord Huntingdon is my real father."

"I apologize. Your blood father, then?"

"No. I got the impression that they were happy to share the story with me but did not want to go further with it. That was fine with me because my father never treated me any differently than my brothers."

Lottie sat and pondered that information. Then she said, "Do your brothers know?"

"No. Father and Mother asked me to keep it to myself. There really was no reason to shame her in their eyes."

Carter waited a few minutes, then said, "Lottie, please come home with me. We need to talk this out, and poor Pamela is probably wandering the streets wondering when she can reclaim her home."

Still reeling under the news Carter had just shared with her, she nodded. "Very well. Let's return to our home and talk this out."

They found Pamela strolling up the street as they left the boarding house. "You may return home now," Lottie said with a grin. "Thank you for letting me stay here when I needed a shoulder to cry on."

"I will always have a shoulder for you, Lottie." Pamela hugged her and waved at Carter who was signaling his driver.

They remained silent on the trip home. Lottie sat across from him and watched the houses and stores as they rode by. Carter studied his hands and appeared to be deep in thought.

Hand-in-hand they climbed the steps to their townhouse and went inside.

"Sir, a wire has arrived for you while you were gone." Milton held out the pale-yellow envelope to him.

"Thank you." Carter took the envelope and followed Lottie to the drawing room. He turned to his butler. "Will you please have cook send in a decent breakfast? Let us know when it is ready, and we'll move to the dining room."

Milton bowed and left them.

"Who is the wire from?" Lottie settled on the sofa.

Carter read the information and then looked up at her. "My mother and father will be arriving tonight."

15

LOTTIE PACED THEIR BEDCHAMBER, HER STOMACH IN KNOTS AND on the verge of bringing up the little bit of food she'd eaten that day. It was about twenty minutes past the time the last train from London would arrive in Bath. That had to be the train Carter's parents were on.

She'd nearly fainted when he read the wire to her. His parents! Wasn't it bad enough that his obnoxious brother came and insulted her? Now his mother and father came to add to her misery.

Carter had assured her more than once that his parents would not behave like Charles. However, each time he said it she saw the flicker of doubt in his eyes.

"Ah, here is where you are hiding." Carter walked into the bedchamber and held out his hand. She walked to him and he wrapped her in his warm, safe arms.

"I'm not exactly hiding. Well, maybe I am, but I don't know if I can face your parents." She leaned back and studied him. "I still think the best thing is for me to leave and you can seek a divorce. I know it's not easy to get, but I will sign any papers and say anything you want me to."

He placed his hands on either side of her head. "If you leave me, I will follow you. If you go to France, I will be there. I will hire people to find you. I love you Lottie and refuse to spend the rest of my life without you."

Lottie shook her head. "Foolish man."

They both froze as the knocker on the door sounded. Carter kissed her on the lips and smoothed back the hair from her forehead. "Come. We face this together."

Clinging to each other, they made their way down the stairs as an older couple passed through the front door. They looked around and spotted her and Carter on the stairs.

"Oh, my. Here is my beautiful new daughter-in-law. Come and give me a hug." The woman who looked remarkably like Carter held out her arms.

Tears of relief flooded Lottie's eyes as her muscles relaxed. She slowly moved forward, and Lady Huntingdon did, in fact, give her a hug. The pleasant odor of lavender and vanilla drifted from Carter's mother. Lottie breathed in the scent.

She was shorter than Lottie, a woman who would be considered well-rounded. She was still beautiful, with dark brown hair, scattered throughout with silver strands.

Lady Huntingdon leaned back and looked into Lottie's eyes. "I'm so happy my son found someone to love."

Then she turned to Carter, her eyes flashing. "Why was I not invited to my son's wedding?"

Lord Huntingdon placed his hand on Lady Huntingdon's shoulder. "Why don't we all move into the library." Then he turned to Lottie. "Welcome to the family, my dear."

Stunned, Lottie took hold of Carter's hand and they followed his parents to the library. They seemed quite familiar with the layout of the house. Lord Huntingdon went directly to the side bar and poured two brandies. Then he turned to Lottie and his wife. "Would you ladies care for a sherry?"

They both nodded. Now that the tension had left her, Lottie felt a combination of hunger and exhaustion. But more than anything, she felt relief.

"I will have Cook prepare a light repast for us." Lottie stood and pulled the bell to summon the footman. Once she gave instructions she returned to the sofa. Carter reached over and took her hand in his.

"I am waiting for an explanation, Carter. Why were we not invited to your wedding?"

Lottie took a deep breath. "That was my fault, my lady."

Lady Huntingdon waved her hand in the air. "Please don't stand on formality, my dear. You may call me Mother or by my given name, Harriet. But since you have a mother of your own, perhaps Harriet is better."

Lottie's heart thumped at the mention of her mother, but no one looked startled, or upset. And the roof did not fall in.

Harriet continued. "Very few of us have led perfect lives, making no mistakes." She reached over and took her husband's hand. "I'm sure my son shared with you my own indiscretion. Thank God my wonderful husband forgave me and life continued."

Lottie almost laughed since Harriet's 'indiscretion' was sitting alongside her, a flesh and blood man, not a minor thing that one can easily overlook. She was growing more uncomfortable by the minute. Harriet was so open about things that Lottie felt the need to hide. But she merely nodded at the woman.

"If the reason we were not notified of the nuptials was for some silly reason about your family, Lottie, then I will forgive you both. Not because I believe you were correct in doing that, but because you are so very young and inexperienced in the way of the world."

Milton rolled in a tea cart with an array of sandwiches and

sweets. Lottie felt her stomach growl and hoped no one else could hear it.

Happy for the interruption, she instructed the butler to place the tea cart next to her. Thank goodness for her years of training because she was able to pour tea, fix it the way each one wanted it, and place a few sandwiches and sweets on the plates she passed around with no visible shaking.

"My dear, you are so gracious and elegant and handled that so well. It must be all that wonderful training you had." Harriet took a bite of a small sandwich and closed her eyes making a light moaning sound. "I have always loved Carter's cook. I would love to steal her, but she won't move to London."

Lord Huntingdon stood. "I don't know about you son, but instead of tea, I believe I will indulge in a bit more brandy. He held up his empty glass. Care to join me?"

"Yes, sir. That sounds perfect." Carter joined his father at the sidebar where they began a conversation about politics.

Lottie was still reeling from the way the visit was going when she realized Harriet had said something that didn't make sense.

"Excuse me, my lady—"

"—Harriet, please."

"Yes. Sorry. You mentioned the training I had. I'm not sure what you mean by that."

She patted her lips with her napkin and smiled. "Well, I know all about you, my dear. Your early life in the countryside, at school in France, and your time here in Bath."

Lottie stared at the woman with her mouth agape. "How . . ." She shook her head "How do you know that?"

Harriet offered her a warm smile and popped a piece of a lemon tart into her mouth just as Carter and Lord Huntingdon joined them again. She swallowed the sweet and patted her mouth again. "Why from speaking with your mother, of course."

Carter choked on his sip of brandy and proceeded to cough until his eyes teared. His parents had him at sixes and sevens since they walked in the door. While he was not as anxious as Lottie had been awaiting their visit, he did have some concerns about what Lottie would do if his parents denounced her, like Charles had. And he did not relish the idea of fisticuffs with his father and then throwing them out of his house.

However, given his mother's history, he would have been very surprised if they did behave badly. He was quite happy that he'd told Lottie about his mother's affair, so she wasn't befuddled by his mother's statement.

"You spoke with Lottie's mother?" He finally got the words out. Lottie just sat there dumbstruck.

Mother had the nerve to raise her eyebrows and act surprised. "Well, of course. When my son presents me with a lovely new daughter-in-law, I certainly want to speak with her family. Make sure they feel welcomed."

Lottie finally came out of her stupor. The grip on his hand could break his bones. "My lady—err, Harriet—I don't know what to say. To say I am surprised is so underwhelming that I, frankly, don't know what to say." Lottie seemed to fumble, trying to get the words out. She looked over at him. "I said 'say' too many times, didn't I?"

He understood since he felt the same way.

"Lottie, dear." His mother stopped and considered for a moment. "I understand your mother prefers Charlotte."

Lottie nodded. "Yes, I changed my name from Charlotte to Lottie when I moved to Bath."

"However, your mother was most distressed to learn you had married without inviting her, either." Mother frowned and Carter almost laughed at the look on his wife's face. She looked like a small child taking a reprimand from her nurse.

"Did my mother tell you we are estranged?"

His mother again waved away her statement. "No matter. A mother is a mother." She looked directly into Lottie's eyes. "Forever."

"My dear, I think any further conversation should be put off until tomorrow." His father placed his glass on the small table alongside him. "I know I am fatigued from the journey here, and it looks like everyone else can use some time to rest. We can continue this conversation in the morning."

He looked at Lottie. "I don't wish to insult my new daughter-in-law but my dear child you look exhausted."

Carter glanced at Lottie, who indeed did look as though she was about to collapse. "I believe you are right, Father." Carter stood and helped Lottie up. His father and mother immediately rose as well, and they all headed toward the stairs.

Mother stood on her tiptoes and kissed him on the cheek. "Good night, son." She touched Lottie's cheek. "And you too, Lottie." Then taking Father's arm she made her way up the stairs. When she reached the top, she looked down at Carter and Lottie. "The usual bedchamber, son?"

"Yes. Mother. The same one."

Carter placed his arm around Lottie's shoulders as they made their way up the stairs. "They use the same bedchamber whenever they visit. But if you want to change that, please feel free. This is your house now."

Once he closed their bedchamber, Lottie collapsed on the bed. "I don't believe it."

Carter loosened his ascot and drew it off. "Which part of this unbelievable night do you not believe?"

"You are correct. The entire night has been surreal." Lottie groaned as she climbed from the bed and presented Carter with her back so he could unfasten her dress.

They slowly removed their clothes, just dropping them where they stood, then climbed into bed and snuggled against each other. "I may sleep for two days." Lottie yawned.

"Me, too."

THE NEXT MORNING CARTER LEFT A SLEEPING LOTTIE IN BED and joined his parents in the breakfast room. "Good morning, Mother, Father."

He took the seat at the head of the table and poured coffee into his cup and took a sip. "Lottie is still sleeping. I don't mind telling you that she was quite anxious awaiting your visit." He reached for the platter of food in the center of the table and filled his plate. "Were you aware of Charles's visit the day before yesterday?"

"Yes. The ninnyhammer! How dare he come to your home and denigrate your wife? When he arrived at our house yesterday and told us what happened, I almost blackened his other eye." Mother in a fury was a sight to behold.

Carter grinned and traded amused glances with his father. They had both at one time or another felt the sting of her displeasure.

Mother laid her hand over Carter's. "You might face some criticism from time to time, son, but please try your best to protect that lovely wife of yours from hearing it. Soon it will all die down anyway, and some new scandal will surface to keep everyone happily engaged in sordidness."

"I am just grateful that we don't live in the middle of

London, where with the Season going on, things would be much more difficult for Lottie."

"She seems like a lovely young lady, Carter." His mother smiled warmly at him. His father nodded.

"Yes. She is. Lottie is kind, caring, smart, but unfortunately due to her restricted upbringing she is not familiar with the ways of the world."

"I sensed that from my conversation with Mrs. Danforth." Mother spread jelly on her toast as she considered her next words. "I must admit I was a bit taken aback when we learned you had married Lottie."

Carter felt himself stiffen, waiting for the condemnation.

"Stop looking so angry, son. I have no intention of denouncing you for this. Every mother wants her children to be happy, and one of the best chances for happiness is to marry someone you love.

"It is obvious from the way you look at Lottie and how you defend her so strongly that she has stolen your heart."

Carter nodded and smiled, thinking about Lottie and how much he cared for her. Had cared for her almost from the moment they had first met. "Yes. I just want her to feel loved and secure. That she can go about in Society—if she wishes— and not be made to feel inferior, since she had absolutely nothing to do with why she is being shunned."

"You're a good man, Carter." His father cleared his throat. "Don't ever turn your back on her like I did with your mother. As much as I love you, and have always loved you, had I been diligent enough in caring for your mother, she would never have had a reason to look elsewhere for affection."

Mother patted the corners of her eyes and reached over to rest her hand on Father's hand.

"Good morning." Lottie entered the room, a vision in loveliness. She must have risen right after he left because she was dressed, her hair fixed, and looking ready to face the day. The glow on her face was something he hadn't seen in a while.

"Good morning, my love." He stood and embraced her, giving her a soft kiss on her cheek.

Lottie greeted his parents and took the seat across from him. She poured tea into her cup and picked up a piece of toast. Mother looked over at her and drew herself up. He wasn't too happy with the look in her eyes. He'd seen it too many times before.

"Lottie, dear. There is one thing I would like you to do." She placed her napkin alongside her place and folded her hands in her lap, looking very innocent, which did not fool Carter at all.

It apparently fooled Lottie though. "Certainly, Harriet." She smiled at his mother.

"Have Carter take you to London and visit with your mother. She has a lot of information that you are unaware of and need to know."

16

"I don't think this is a good idea." Lottie twisted the handkerchief in her hand as she and Carter made their way to her mother's house. They had secured a hackney after leaving the train from Bath to London. The vehicle swayed as it rode over ruts in the road, then was stopped for a while in traffic.

So as not to give her mother heart failure, she'd sent her a wire announcing their visit. She also did not want to arrive at her mother's house while she entertained a 'customer.'

"Not so. This is a very good idea. You will never be content with your life until you face your mother and hear what she has to say." Carter had been trying to keep her calm since she had decided to make the visit. Lady Huntingdon had been quite insistent that a talk with her mother was something she needed to do. Besides that, she missed Mama very much.

She twisted the handkerchief some more and looked out the window. Since she'd only been to her mother's house once before, on the day of that horrendous visit, she had no idea how close they were.

"You're a strong woman and you can do this." Carter

moved across the space and sat alongside her, pulling her against his side. "Whatever happens, I am here with you."

And that was perhaps the only thing that kept her from fleeing the carriage and running back to the train station. Carter was her anchor in a whirlwind of emotions. She loved him so much and found it hard to believe he loved her back.

Five minutes later, the carriage stopped in front of what she recognized as her mother's door. Her heart began to pound, and her stomach muscles cramped. "I can't do this."

"Yes. You can." Carter jumped out first and turned to help her out. She hesitated and he raised his eyebrows.

"All right." She slid forward on the seat and took his hand. Together they climbed the steps and before they even reached the top step, the door opened. Not by the man she remembered from before, but by her mother.

Mama looked tired and had lost some weight. Before they could even greet each other, a man stepped up behind her and put his hand on her shoulder.

He was an older man, with black and silver hair and twinkling blue eyes. Had she not met him here she might have even liked him. His smile was warm and genuine. But he was here in Mama's house, even though she knew Lottie was coming for a visit.

Lottie turned to go back down the steps when Mama said. "Wait, Charlotte. Please."

Carter took two steps down to where she was and took her hand. "We've come all this way, sweetheart."

Taking a deep breath, she walked back up the steps and entered the house.

Her hands twisting, Mama said, "I have tea and sandwiches in the drawing room."

Lottie nodded and waited for her mother to proceed.

Having only visited once, she had no memory of where the drawing room was.

The four of them walked down the corridor and turned into what Lottie remembered as the room where the party had been held. She shuddered and Carter squeezed her hand.

Once they were all seated, Mama said, "You look good, Charlotte. It appears marriage agrees with you." Her voice was steady and calm, but her paleness and how tightly she clasped her fingers in her lap told a different story.

Lottie bit her tongue with the sharp retort she had. Since everyone was so adamant that they have this talk, she might as well remain cordial. Mama could have her say, and she and Carter would leave on the next train to Bath.

Carter had mentioned that he'd notified his staff at his London house that they might be spending the night. She doubted it, but it was probably best to have somewhere to go if the 'visit' lasted longer than she expected it would.

"Thank you, Mama. Marriage does agree with me." She turned to Carter and saw the love and caring in his eyes and almost cried. But then her emotions were running rampant at the moment.

"Allow me to introduce Mr. Franklin Monroe." Mama's eyes lit up when she turned to the man seated next to her. Lottie felt as though she wanted to bring up her breakfast.

"I am pleased to meet you, Mrs. Westbrooke." Mr. Monroe smiled at her and Lottie wanted to scream. They were all acting so normal, so different from what she had expected. What she had expected she didn't really know, but this very dignified man seated next to Mama was not part of her imaginings.

Lottie nodded and gestured to Carter. "My husband, Mr. Carter Westbrooke."

Mr. Monroe rose and shook Carter's hand. "A pleasure to meet you, Mr. Westbrooke."

Carter nodded. "A pleasure."

My, aren't we all being so very prim and proper.

They fell silent and Mama waved at the tea cart. "Tea?"

"Yes. Thank you." Lottie wanted anything to prevent conversation between them all. She still couldn't understand why Mama had Mr. Monroe join her for this visit.

"Young man, it's well past the noon hour. Would you care for a brandy instead of tea?" Mr. Monroe stood and addressed Carter.

"Yes. Actually, a brandy sounds good."

Lottie was not surprised to see Mr. Monroe acting as host. He apparently had some status here. He poured two brandies and brought one over to Carter.

Mama began to pour tea for her and Lottie. She was as graceful as she remembered, her delicate hands deftly pouring, adding sugar and cream and passing the cup to Lottie.

She then filled a small plate with a few sandwiches and passed them around. Lottie was happy to have the tea, but with her stomach in knots, she didn't think she would be able to consume food for days.

Once again silence reigned. The men sipping their brandies, the women their tea, and everyone pretending they were enjoying their plate of sandwiches.

Mama looked over at Mr. Monroe. Knowing her mother so well, Lottie recognized her plea for help.

Mr. Monroe cleared his throat. "I would like to say that as of last month, your lovely and charming mother has become my betrothed."

It was then that Lottie looked at her mother's hand and noticed the tasteful diamond and ruby ring. "Betrothed?"

That statement stunned her almost as much as when Lady

Huntingdon told her she'd spoke with her mother. Was she to be stunned and surprised again?

Most likely.

"Congratulations, Mr. Monroe," Carter said and raised his brandy glass to them. "Mrs. Danforth, I wish you happiness."

Lottie just stared. She felt as though she was in a play where everyone knew their lines, but she didn't even know what part she played.

"Charlotte, I am prepared to answer any questions you have." Mama patted Mr. Monroe's hand and continued. "Franklin knows everything there is to know about me, so please don't hold back.

"We should have had this conversation a long time ago, and I blame myself every day for you learning about my life the way you did, forcing you to flee."

"Go ahead, honey," Carter said as he took her hand in his.

Well, if Mama wasn't uncomfortable with everyone in the room hearing what she had to say, then Lottie was going to find out everything she thought about over the past year.

"Very well. Let's start with my father. Do you even know who he is?"

Mama cringed and Mr. Monroe put his arm around her shoulders. That seemed to settle her. "Yes. Your father was Mr. Jerome Danvers."

She took a deep breath. "My husband."

The loud ticking of the longcase clock in the corner kept beat with Lottie's heart. Both the clock and the pounding of her heart drowned out all sound. She just continued to stare at her mother. "You were married?"

"Yes."

"I am legitimate?"

"Yes."

"Why didn't you tell me? When I asked over the years

about my father you told me about him. But since last year, I assumed you made that all up."

"No. He was a wonderful man who died too young."

Hundreds of questions raced around her mind. So many she didn't even know where to start.

"Mrs. Danforth, perhaps it would be best if you started at the beginning and told Lottie what she needs to know." Carter looked over at Lottie. "My wife looks a bit shocked right now, and I think just hearing your story would help."

Mr. Monroe nodded in Mama's direction and she began her story.

Carter took the clean handkerchief from his pocket and handed it to Lottie since the one she held was almost shredded.

Mama began to speak, her voice very soft. "Your father and I were quite young when we married. We also married against his parents' approval. I was the daughter of the local baker and his parents were landowners. Gentry.

"We were young, and in love, and very happy. Your father made his living by painting portraits."

"My father was an artist?" Lottie turned to Carter. "I have no talent in that area."

"Not so, my dear. I've seen your watercolors."

"When he died," Mrs. Danforth continued, "my parents were already gone, and his parents would have nothing to do with me. That was the same week I discovered I was expecting you.

"I took a job as a maid until my employer discovered I was carrying a baby and he fired me."

"Nicely done of the man to toss out a woman who had no one and a baby on the way," Carter said.

Mr. Monroe nodded his approval.

"I took in laundry and sewing until you were born. It didn't pay much, but I was able to keep myself fed. At that time, I was living in an abandoned hunting lodge."

Mrs. Danforth drew in a deep breath and Mr. Monroe took her hand in his. "A man in the small village where we were living heard of my plight and offered me a job as a wet nurse to his newborn son. He was married but separated from his wife who lived in London. He, however, had the child with him.

"It came to a point where he gave me an ultimatum. Either become his mistress or he would throw me out. At the time, I felt I had no choice. Maybe I did, but I was so very tired, and I wanted so much to provide more than the absolute necessities for you."

"What happened to him?"

"He grew tired of me, which happens. He set me up with a house in London and secured another protector for me. That was when I arranged for you to live with the Stevens, who I knew from my childhood." She looked Lottie in the eye. "Over the years I've had only five protectors."

"Four, my dear," Mr. Monroe said. "I will soon be your husband."

Mrs. Danforth looked at the man with such love in her eyes Lottie felt her own tear up.

Without thinking, the words came tumbling out of her mouth. "Why does everyone think you are such a notorious . . ."

"Courtesan," Mrs. Danforth said, offering Lottie a soft smile. "Because of my parties. I love having music, conversation, and stimulating evenings. I enjoy inviting poets to read and lectures on books and timely events. I even secured an opera singer from Italy one time."

Mr. Monroe cleared his throat. "May I add that I met your mother five years ago. My wife, at the time, was suffering from a mental problem and had been in hospital for years."

He looked at Mama. "We fell in love but could do nothing about it. Last month, my wife took her own life. I immediately proposed to your mother and she accepted. After another month or so, we will be wed."

Lottie leaned back on the sofa where they sat and stared at her mother. This past year she'd thought so many terrible things about this woman. Would Lottie have made the choices she made? It was hard to say because her mother made sure she lived the sort of life that would prevent her from ever being in a position to have to make that sort of a decision.

"One thing I want you to know, Charlotte. I love you more than you will ever know. Well, maybe not. Once you have a child of your own and hold him or her in your arms you will understand how I feel about you." By the end of her state-ment, she and Mama were both crying.

They both rose and embraced, hugging, crying, and she was sure, making the two men in the room a tad uncom-fortable.

After a few minutes, they wiped their faces and sat side by side on the sofa, holding hands. Carter moved over to one of the chairs to give them more room.

"Charlotte, please tell me this nonsense between us has ended."

"Yes, Mama, I missed you so much." She laid her head on her mother's shoulder as she'd done so many times as a young girl.

"As I missed you."

Mr. Monroe looked over at Mama. "My dear, why don't you tell them about tomorrow evening?"

Mama clapped her hands like a young girl and Lottie sat up. "Oh, yes. Lord and Lady Huntingdon have invited the four of us to dinner tomorrow night as a celebration of your wedding and our engagement."

Lottie didn't think she could take any more surprises. Her mother-in-law was breaking every rule of the ton by accepting a courtesan into her home. To sit at her dining room table.

"Your mother is a remarkable woman," Mama said to Carter.

"As are you, as well," Carter replied.

The two couples chatted for hours, catching up on what Lottie had been doing in Bath. Lottie still had a few more questions for her mother, but once the evening grew to an end, she felt as though she knew everything she needed to know.

Most of which was how much her mother loved her and all the decisions she'd made had been to provide a better life for Lottie.

Lottie and Carter left for their house in London after a lovely dinner with Mama and Mr. Monroe, who Lottie found to be a wonderful gentleman. A shipping line owner, Mr. Monroe was charming, humorous, and very much in love with her mother.

He told them at dinner that he was selling his business so he and Mama could travel. Then they would buy a house and enjoy the rest of their lives. Lottie immediately mentioned all the wonderful houses in Bath. They all laughed.

As they were undressing for bed, Carter suddenly burst out laughing.

"What?"

"It just occurred to me. You've been thinking you're not good enough for me because of your background."

"Yes?"

He sat alongside her on the bed while she untied the ribbons holding up her stockings. "Legally, I am not a bastard, but in reality, I am because my parents were not married to each other. You, on the other hand, are perfectly legitimate."

Lottie turned and stared at him, her mouth agape. "You are correct. How odd."

"Odd, but funny." He pulled her down onto the bed where he kissed her, and she kissed him back with all the love in her heart.

EPILOGUE

Four months later

"MAMA, I'M FINE. I STILL HAVE ANOTHER FEW MONTHS BEFORE the babe arrives. You and Carter are driving me crazy." Lottie shifted on the sofa and attempted to rise but fell back.

Her mother fluttered around her like a bird. "See. You should be resting more."

"Resting from what? All I do is eat and rest." The child she was carrying would be huge when it finally arrived. He would probably come out walking and demanding meat pies.

"Is she giving you problems again, Alice?" Mr. Monroe, who had been asking Lottie to call him Papa since the day he and her mother married, entered the drawing room with Carter right behind him. He leaned over and kissed her mother on the cheek.

Lottie had grown to love her stepfather over the past few months but still wasn't quite ready to call him Papa. Since she'd never had a father, the word just stuck on her tongue. So, she did what anyone else would be in that situation. She waited until he looked at her before she asked him anything.

Her mother and her new husband had moved to a lovely house only a few blocks from them in Bath once they had returned from their wedding trip. The new Mrs. Monroe joined Lottie and Carter's church, and no one seemed to know —or care—who she had been in London. She had a feeling that Carter and his persuasive abilities had something to do with that.

"Yes, she won't sit still," Mama said as Mr. Monroe joined her on the sofa.

Carter sat on the arm of the chair and took Lottie's hand. "Feeling a bit restless, are you?"

To her horror she burst into tears. "I feel so fat, so unwieldly." She took the handkerchief that Carter placed into her hand. He always seemed to have more than one on his person all the time.

"Why don't we send for tea?" Her stepfather said.

Lottie cried harder. "Then I'll be even fatter than I am now."

Carter stood and took Lottie's hand. "Up you go, sweetheart. Time for a nap." He walked her out of the room, rubbing her back as she lumbered alongside him.

Once her husband had her settled in bed, he sat next to her. "Has there been any news from Pamela?"

Lottie shook her head. "No. Not since her visit here last week." She sniffed and wiped her nose. "I am concerned about her."

The week before, Pamela had shown up one evening in a very agitated state. She told Lottie that she had some difficulty that only one person could help her with, and she would be unable to visit with her or Addie for a while until it was resolved.

With no more information than that, Pamela had kissed

her on the cheek and told her she hoped to be back when the baby was born.

Neither she nor Addie had heard anything from her since.

"Do you suppose there is more than one baby in here?" Lottie asked.

Carter turned quite pale. "You mean twins?"

"Yes." Lottie rested her hand on her stomach and said, "A few times I swear I felt the baby kick in two different places."

"Well the child has two feet."

"However, unless your son has *four* feet, I keep thinking there is more than one."

Carter stood walked to the window and drew the drapes. "Don't worry about that now. Just take a nice nap and you'll feel better about everything when you wake up."

He kissed her on the head and moved to the door. Just as his hand touched the latch, she said, "Four feet. I'm sure of it."

The End

Did you like this story? Please consider leaving a review on either Goodreads or the place where you bought it. Long or short, your review will help other readers discover new authors and make purchasing decisions!

I hope you had fun reading Lottie and Carter's love story. Coming next in The Misfits of Bath series: *Lady Pamela and the Gambler*.

Miss Adeline Mallory, who has suffered from dyslexia her whole life convinces her parents that marriage is simply not in her future and to release her dowry to her so she can open a bookstore.

Miss Charlotte Danvers escapes the reputation her mother built as the most expensive courtesan in London and supports herself by teaching young ladies all the finer points of the ton who will never accept her as one of their own.

Lady Pamela Manning cannot get through an entire sentence without stuttering. But she sings like an angel. She's happy with her new life as a music teacher, even if most of her students have no ear for music.

Get your copy on Amazon.
You can find a list of all my books here: http://
calliehutton.com/books/
PIX
For the special treat I promised you,
click here to receive a free copy of
A Little Bit of Romance, three short stories of lovers reunited.
Enjoy!
https://www.subscribepage.com/f3b6d8_copy

ABOUT THE AUTHOR

Callie Hutton, the *USA Today* bestselling author of *The Elusive Wife*, writes both Western Historical and Regency romance, with "historic elements and sensory details" (*The Romance Reviews*). She also pens an occasional contemporary or two. Callie lives in Oklahoma with several rescue dogs and her top cheerleader husband of many years. Her family also includes her daughter, son, daughter-in-law and twin grandsons affectionately known as "The Twinadoes."

Callie loves to hear from readers. Contact her directly at calliehutton11@gmail.com or find her online at http://calliehutton.com/ . Sign up for her newsletter to receive information on new releases, appearances, contests and exclusive subscriber content. Visit her on Facebook, Twitter and Goodreads.

Callie Hutton has written more than thirty books. For a complete listing, go to www.calliehutton.com/books

Praise for books by Callie Hutton

A Wife by Christmas

"A *Wife by Christmas* is the reason why we read romance...the perfect story for any season." --The Romance Reviews Top Pick

The Elusive Wife

"I loved this book and you will too. Jason is a hottie & Oliva is the kind of woman we'd all want as a friend. Read it!" --Cocktails and Books

"In my experience I've had a few hits but more misses with historical romance so I was really pleasantly surprised to be hooked from the start by obviously good writing." --Book Chick City

"The historic elements and sensory details of each scene make the story come to life, and certainly helps immerse the reader in the world that Olivia and Jason share." --The Romance Reviews

"You will not want to miss *The Elusive Wife*." --My Book Addiction

"...it was a well written plot and the characters were likeable." --Night Owl Reviews

A Run for Love

"An exciting, heart-warming Western love story!" *--NY Times* bestselling author Georgina Gentry

"I loved this book!!! I read the BEST historical romance last night...It's called *A Run For Love.*" *--NY Times* bestselling author Sharon Sala

"This is my first Callie Hutton story, but it certainly won't be my last." --The Romance Reviews

A Prescription for Love

"There was love, romance, angst, some darkness, laughter, hope and despair." --RomCon

"I laughed out loud at some of the dialogue and situations. I think you will enjoy this story by Callie Hutton." --Night Owl Reviews

An Angel in the Mail

"...a warm fuzzy sensuous read. I didn't put it down until I was done." --Sizzling Hot Reviews

Visit www.calliehutton.com for more information.

Printed in Great Britain
by Amazon